VENGEANCE FROM BEYOND

THE GHOST REAPERS SERIES

BOOK 3

IAN FORTEY

AND

RON RIPLEY

EDITED BY ANNE LAO
AND DAWN KLEMISH

ISBN: 979-8-89476-277-7
Copyright © 2024 by ScareStreet.com

Enter the Realm of Terror...

We'd like to take a moment to thank you for your support and invite you to join our VIP newsletter.

Dive deeper into the darkness with exclusive offers, early access to new releases, and bone-chilling deals when you sign up at www.ScareStreet.com.

Let the nightmares begin...

See you in the shadows,
Scare Street

PROLOGUE

When the moon is full, Siyah Lake alongside Merkara Base looks like the blackest oil. The lake is situated in the shallowest of valleys such that the wind seems to avoid touching it. The water will remain still except in the strongest of storms. It looks like a giant sleeping thing, and you get the sense that it's poised and ready to strike at any moment.

Sometimes, when it's late enough and it's quiet as a grave, a Siberian crane might take flight from the water's edge, its soft wings beating for just a moment until the silence returns. It's as if the darkness woke for a moment and then returned to its slumber.

Lieutenant Colonel Willard Branson walked along the shore of the lake almost every night. He had dealt with insomnia for years and had long ago given up trying to force himself to sleep. The walks helped sometimes, but there was no guarantee. He might go home and sleep, or he might go home and stare at the ceiling. He had also long ago given up caring about that.

Branson had been the commanding officer at the Merkara Base in Turkey for nearly ten years. The NATO base was home to the 619th Air Base Squadron, which aided missions in Europe and the Middle East.

His appointment had come as a surprise; he'd heard rumors of at least three others ahead of him in line for the job. He was grateful for it, though, and had, for the most part, enjoyed and taken pride in the work he did. It could be harrowing and stressful at times, but that was the job.

He had grown to love Turkey. He had been stationed in many places over the years that were not nearly as enjoyable, so there was something to be said for that. Still, it was far from a vacation.

Tensions in nearby Vakovia had steadily increased for months. Word came down the pipe that American mercenaries supporting the President had attempted an assassination of his biggest political rival. It had set off a storm in the region.

Branson wanted to focus on his work—keep the base running smoothly, follow orders, do what needed to be done—but there was a lot of chatter about Reaper Company. It made everyone look bad. He kept a lid on it as best he could, but there was no way to stop the rumor mill, and he knew it would look worse to try.

"You seem lost in thought," Janet said softly.

The wife walked next to him while he walked their Irish setter, Ptolemy. The dog was used to these late-night walks and enjoyed wandering the lakeshore looking for waterfowl and frogs.

"Just thinking," he told her.

They had celebrated twenty-five years of marriage the autumn before. He was glad to have her with him now as things were holding together so tenuously.

"Clearly," she said, teasing him. "This Vakovia stuff again? I thought it was all cleaned up."

"Not at all *clean*, no," he said.

She knew there were some things he was allowed to talk about with her and some things he was supposed to keep secret. He never followed those rules with her. The situation in Vakovia was a bit of a gray area. So much was already in the press, but other aspects were still kept under wraps by the brass.

"You're not going to have to send anyone over there, are you?" she asked.

"Doubtful. But tensions all around are still…"

"American mercenaries are American soldiers in the eyes of most. I know," she said.

It was unfortunately true. It didn't matter that the Reapers were

2

unsanctioned. They had military weapons and a military budget. For most people in the region, to hear the American government deny they had anything to do with the Reapers was just a bald-faced lie. Branson wished he could stay out of all of it.

They finished their walk along the lake's edge and returned home, their house the last one on the street and the farthest from the noise and activity that sprung up once the sun rose.

"I'm heading upstairs for a moment. Are you going to have a cup of tea?" she asked.

"I think so," he replied, bending over to take off the dog's harness and hang up his leash.

Ptolemy wandered off to his bed and flopped on his pillow in the living room. Branson headed to the kitchen and put on the kettle, found his favorite cup, and dropped a tea bag and a spoonful of sugar into it.

He waited until the water in the kettle had hit a rolling boil. Branson filled his cup carefully and then waited another moment before adding a splash of milk.

Janet had not returned, so he walked carefully, holding the small cup by the handle as he went in search of her.

"Tea's ready, hon. You coming back down, or should I go up?" he called at the foot of the stairs.

His wife did not reply. Branson leaned his head over the railing and looked up at the second floor.

"Janet?"

Still no response. Branson set the teacup down hastily and made his way to his office just a few steps away. He unlocked the top drawer of his desk and pulled out his service pistol. He loaded it quickly and returned to the stairs.

"I'll be up in a few minutes," he shouted as he started his way up the steps.

He had not endured any threats to his person on the base, but he was ready for anything. There was no reason for his wife to not respond. More than anyone he knew, she should not have been in danger, but this Reaper Company business had him on edge.

The bathroom light was on, but she was not inside when he gave it a quick check. He maneuvered slowly toward the bedroom door, which was closed when it should not have been.

He had been away from his wife for so many years before. His job simply hadn't allowed him to spend time with his wife the way he wanted to. So many moments were lost to his duty. Birthdays, Christmases, all of those days he should have been with her.

When she started feeling sick, he got some time away from the base to go see her, but no amount of leave would have lasted long enough. Her condition only worsened as the days went on. He violated a direct order to head back to Turkey by staying at her bedside on that last day.

The general had called him personally and told him he needed to go. Branson had told the general he could court-martial him, but he was not going to leave his wife's side. She was dead four hours later.

When she came back to him, it was like a dream. To have that chance all over again, to be with her anywhere, forever, was more than he could have hoped.

Janet was not angry. She didn't hate him for missing all that time. She just felt the same sorrow he had and had the same hope that going forward, things would be different.

Things were different after he learned that if he had her wedding ring, as cold as ice, she could come with him wherever he went. He never had to sacrifice time with her ever again.

No one else on the base could see her, but no one else could know that she was with him, either. It was a difficult adjustment to act like she wasn't there when others were around and to not speak directly to her when others could overhear. He didn't want to come off like a crazy person because no one would entrust command of a military facility to a man who talked to his dead wife.

Having her with him had been invaluable. She was someone he could speak to about everything, and he knew his secrets would always be safe. Plus, Janet had a way of understanding things. She had always been smarter than he was. She also had greater insight and a more refined way of looking at almost any situation.

Reaper Company had put him on edge. Those men worked with the dead. They could see them, and that was a problem. He didn't need anyone showing up at Merkara who could see Janet.

Worse were the rumors he had heard about someone laying waste to Reaper Company. A man in Vakovia could kill the dead. Branson had told Janet nothing about him; he didn't want her to know that someone out there could take her away from him.

Back when Reaper Company was formed, Branson was involved in the initial planning. A select few knew he could see and speak with the dead. It was never something that he had made public in the military, but he had slipped up somewhere along the line. Some people kept tabs on everyone, it seemed. And the dead liked to talk to one another. Someone had outed him, and he was brought into the fold.

His involvement had ended quickly, and for a time, he thought the idea had folded.

The name Reaper Company meant nothing to him at first, but he was eventually able to put the pieces together. He still wasn't sure when they became active, or what jobs they did, but they were not as much of a surprise to him as they were to others.

Branson took a deep breath and turned the bedroom doorknob with his free hand. The door fell open as he stepped in with his gun raised.

A bedside lamp provided the only light in the room, but an article of clothing had been tossed over it. Janet was at the foot of the bed facing him, her eyes wide. The man's hand across her mouth prevented her from speaking. A second hand was atop her head.

Branson lowered his gun several inches, confused by the sight. He had not been able to touch his wife in years. When he tried, his hand merely passed through an unobstructed cold patch in the air. The effect was the same when she tried to touch him. And yet, this strange man…

He looked out from behind Janet, and Branson could see that he was bald and scarred. This was the man from Vakovia. The man who killed the dead.

"Lt. Col. Branson," the man said calmly.

He took his hand slowly from Janet's mouth and held it at the side of her head. Both hands kept a firm grip, and he looked as though he might pull Janet's head from her shoulders.

"Shane Ryan," Branson replied.

"You know me; good. That'll make this easier."

"I read your file after the Vakovian government cleared you."

"And I read a file on you," Shane replied. "Said you were one of the founding fathers of Reaper Company. And here you are in Turkey, just a snowball's throw from where your men spent a month trying to kill me."

"What is he talking about?" Janet asked.

Branson ignored his wife.

"It's not true. I was brought in before it had a name. Before there was a group, when it was just an idea. Myself and others who could communicate with ghosts. But I dropped out before anything became solid. I saw it for what it was."

Shane's hands did not waver. He held Janet as if she were still real flesh and blood. Branson could see how his grip messed her hair and pulled at her face.

"Well, tell me, Colonel. What was it?"

"A mistake. Treason. A goddamn nightmare. I had no part in whatever it is right now; you have my word."

Shane stared at him for a long moment as though weighing his words.

"This your wife?" he asked.

"I am Janet Branson, and I am his wife, thank you," she answered angrily. Shane smiled.

"Apologies, ma'am. It's just that I'd been led to believe your husband had been trying to murder me for a number of weeks now. And that he murdered several men I knew."

"And how many men have *you* murdered, Ryan?" Branson countered.

"Somewhere close to sixty, I think," Shane answered simply. "They could have stopped at any time. I was the one trying to get away."

"Will was not involved; you heard him," Janet said. The fire she'd had when she was alive had only grown since she'd returned as a spirit. She did not play meek.

"I did hear that," Shane agreed. "But I also heard you were pulled in at the beginning. So who did the pulling, Branson? Who killed my friends? Who's been trying to kill me?"

"I'm not telling you anything until you let my wife go," Branson replied.

Shane smiled again.

"You'd better tell me something. My hands are getting awfully cold, and I'm going to have to do something soon."

CHAPTER 1
HOME

Shane's plane landed at Logan International Airport just after nine o'clock in the morning. The Vakovians had arranged for his flight home to Boston as well as his quick stopover in Turkey. To the best of his knowledge, his name had been fully cleared, and the incidents were blamed on Reaper Company.

The articles that Shane had read made it clear that the mercenary group was not sanctioned by any government and had instead been employed by the former Vakovian President before his untimely death in a helicopter crash.

That was all well and good on the surface, but none of it fixed the problem. Reaper Company still existed, and someone was giving orders. Shane took particular issue with the orders to kill him.

The group might have been out of Vakovia, but Shane knew it was probably still operating in several countries. The Reapers were making money, ignoring laws, and wreaking havoc wherever they went. Anyone bold enough to stand against them would probably die.

Governments could threaten the Reapers with sanctions and arrests, but the Reapers were running their show with spectral assets. Ghostly assassins didn't need to worry about the rule of law or the UN or military justice. They'd kill whoever got in the way. The Reapers did not need to stop until they wanted to, or someone forced them to, and so far, only Shane fit the bill for the second option.

He had left his car at the airport before leaving the country almost two months earlier and found it covered in fliers. The engine rumbled when he turned the key, and he was happy to be back someplace familiar.

Shane sat still for a long moment, listening to the rumble of the engine before leaning over and opening the glove box. An unopened pack of Lucky Strikes greeted him like an old friend. He pulled it out and lit one, inhaling deeply. He hadn't had a proper cigarette in far too long.

The drive back home took Shane about an hour and a half. Part of him felt like he should have been rushing, should have had his foot heavy on the gas and been chewing up the road. He had been away for too long. But another part of him just wanted to savor the moment. Being alone in the car with a cigarette was something he'd wanted for just as long.

The sun was high in the sky by the time he arrived at the house on Berkley Street. It was a clear day, it was warm, and something was wrong. There was a feeling about the house that wasn't right. It was hard to put his finger on it, but it was definitely there.

He entered the house, and the smell of lavender was stronger than he remembered. He caught hints of something dead beneath it, and the cool air was a relief from the heat outside. Much of his time in Vakovia had been amid a brutal heat wave. The chill of the house was something he missed.

Something hit Shane hard across the leg. He turned in time to see Eloise scowling fiercely, a rage behind her eyes that he had not witnessed in years.

"I thought you were dead!" she spat, the anger in her voice palpable. She wasn't upset or scolding; she was furious.

"I almost was," he replied.

"Men came to the house. Soldiers," Herbert said, appearing through one of the walls. The Davis sisters, Thaddeus, and Carl arrived a moment later, crowding around him and blocking his path.

"They worked with spirits," Carl said.

"Herbert saved me," Thaddeus added as the Davis sisters giggled.

"One of them got lost in the cellar," Daisy said.

"He's still there," Daphne added.

"He'll stay there forever," Dora concluded.

Shane held up his hands to silence everyone.

"Are you all okay?" he asked.

"Of course," Carl answered. "But these men were not alone. They were in radio contact with others. They had been monitoring the house."

"Figures," Shane said. He made his way toward the kitchen while the others followed.

"I used to know a fella not so long ago who talked about working with dead folks in the Army," Daphne said as she followed behind him. Her sisters nodded. "Now, he said he was part of this group called Reaper Company. That ring any bells?"

Shane paused and looked back at the spirit. She and her sisters smiled sweetly.

"You never mentioned that," Carl said.

"You never asked," Dora answered.

"You know Reaper Company?" Shane asked. The sisters shrugged in unison.

"We knew a boy named Joe. Joe Solomon. Was it Joe Solomon?" Daphne said.

"Joe Suleman," Daisy corrected.

"Joe Sullivan," Dora offered. Daphne shrugged.

"Point is, he was one of them for a spell. What he described was an awful lot like the men who came here, soldiers—living men—partnered with ghosts."

Shane put on the kettle for a pot of coffee, listening to the sisters' roundabout way of explaining things.

"How did you meet your friend Joe?" he asked.

"Oh, he wasn't a friend. He was in the hospital with us. He was all kinds of messed up in the head," Daphne answered.

"We ran into lots of folks with bad stories in the hospital," Dora added.

"Some were just bad people," Daisy clarified.

"Yeah, we had to do something about some of them," Daphne finished.

"I see. But you're all okay now, right?"

"The house is as well," Carl answered. "We had to dispatch two spirits that came with them, however."

"Better them than you," Shane said. He poured a cup of coffee and then sat down at the table.

His weeks in exile had been unexpected, as had the news that Reaper Company had come to his house. He drank his coffee and rattled off what he thought were the relevant details of his time away. He explained why he had been gone so long, what had happened while he was there, and what he planned to do going forward as briefly and efficiently as possible.

The ghosts in the house didn't need to know all of his comings and goings, but being away for over a month was unusual. Now, it seemed like they were involved anyway, if Reaper Company had shown intent on taking some of them away while he was gone. It also proved quite handily that they were not done with him. All the more reason for him to not be done with them.

"What did this Colonel Branson tell you?" Carl asked once Shane had brought everyone up to speed.

Shane took a drink of his coffee and looked at Carl for a moment, and then around the room. Seven spirits in his home, all at risk now, thanks to Reaper Company. All of them also heavily invested in his plans and what he'd learned. So much for wanting to handle things on his own.

"I got a name," he answered finally. "Reaper Company is run out of the US. Branson said he was brought in by someone I used to know."

"Who?" Thaddeus blurted out.

"Someone who should know better," Shane replied.

The ghosts in the house didn't need to know more than that. They weren't coming with him on any mission, and the less they knew in the long run, the better. That was true for anyone who wasn't looking to be involved in a problem. If Reaper Company came back when Shane was away, they wouldn't be able to learn anything.

In fairness, Shane didn't expect that Reaper Company would have much luck trying to extract information from Carl or the others. At best, they might be able to escape with their lives, and even that was unlikely. Hopefully, after their first trip to Shane's house, they had learned their lesson.

Colonel Branson had given Shane the name Captain Brett Hawkins. He was Shane's CO for a brief period in Afghanistan. It had not been for Shane's full tour, and Hawkins had come in late to replace the previous CO who had nearly died from an IED.

Hawkins was younger than Shane. He had moved quickly through the ranks, but no one knew much about him. He had served with both Shane and Davis Blakely, however. In retrospect, that couldn't have been a coincidence.

It seemed like there was more going on behind the scenes than Shane realized. For Hawkins to get where he needed to go, to be in such close contact with the people he later recruited into Reaper Company, someone else had to be helping him out.

If Branson was to be believed, the Reapers were now solely under the command of Hawkins. They were not officially affiliated with any military command, and Hawkins ran the show as a civilian.

It could have been as Branson said. Maybe it had started as something the military was sanctioning or looking into. Crazier things had happened. Even the CIA dabbled in the paranormal, mind control, and psychic operatives for a time during the Cold War. The idea that the military would try to make soldiers out of the dead seemed almost reasonable compared to that.

If Branson and others like him had pulled the plug on the project in its infancy, Hawkins could have kept it going on the side. Like others Shane had encountered in Vakovia, maybe Branson simply gave up military life to pursue the money he could get by running a mercenary outfit with ghosts.

Shane didn't care about Hawkins' motivations. His goal was to end it and nothing more. Whether that was out of revenge for what had happened to Blakely, Oleg the Brute, and Radek Dorn, a need for justice, or his personal desire didn't matter. The end result was the same. The world would be a more peaceful and safer place without Reaper Company in it.

"Do you know where to find this person?" Carl asked.

Shane finished his coffee.

"Not yet. But I'll find out."

"Are you sure it's safe?" Daphne asked. "Because it doesn't sound safe. They came to the house, and they made you hide in a cemetery in a foreign country for a month. It sounds dangerous."

"We could come with you," Daisy offered.

"We could kill him," Dora added.

"Real quick, too. It doesn't even have to be messy unless you want it to be messy," Daphne finished.

"I appreciate the offer, but no," Shane said.

The sisters were a little more animated than he was used to. He forgot sometimes that while there was a strange charm to them being identical triplets, and they were almost childlike in the way that they would play with Eloise throughout the house, there was more to them.

The Davis sisters had been in that mental asylum for a reason. And, like most ghosts, their civilized side could give way to something darker at the drop of a hat. It was something Shane was used to from Carl and Eloise, but even when they dropped their more human personas and became like the ghosts he sometimes was forced to destroy, it took a bit of adjusting.

"If you say so. But if they come back to the house, can we kill them?" Daphne asked.

"We'll keep it quiet," Dora said.

"No one has to hear a single scream," Daisy finished.

"By all means," Shane said.

If anyone came to the house, especially someone who knew what was waiting for them, they were choosing their fate, and Shane had no sympathy.

He got up from the table and cleaned his coffee cup before putting it away. He wanted to take a shower and relax for the rest of the day. He had things to do, but he wasn't going to miss his first chance in a long time to get some peaceful rest.

Vakovia had nearly killed him. He'd lost more than twenty pounds living in the wild. He had been battered and beaten more times than he cared to count. He'd nearly exploded, been shot at, drowned, and more. He'd earned at least one day of rest. Plus, it would give him time to plan his next steps.

If Hawkins had left the military to start Reaper Company, he would not be easy to find. Shane would have to turn over some very old stones to find him.

CHAPTER 2
DIGGING UP THE PAST

Shane awoke just after sunrise. His room was bright, and though he felt like he could have slept for another day or two, the sun was unrelenting.

"Are you leaving again?" Eloise asked.

She was staring at him from the foot of the bed. He caught her angry gaze and sat up, running a hand across his smooth head as he stretched his back and arms.

"I am," he answered simply.

"You haven't even been back a whole day yet," she shot back, her tone accusatory.

"I haven't," he agreed.

"What happens if those soldiers return? What if they have a dozen ghosts with them?"

"I trust you to take care of it."

"Don't you patronize me. We've gone over this before. I'm not a child. I'm not going to be brushed aside with silly words. Carl was already kidnapped from this house once, have you forgotten that?"

Her tone was demanding and shrill. She was like an angry mother scolding her child. Shane was willing to give Eloise a lot of leeway in how she conducted herself and how she spoke to him, but there was a limit.

"Do you think I forgot that? Do you think I'm leaving to go play with neighborhood cats or go trick-or-treating?" Shane replied.

He had kept his tone civil and calm, but the digs at Eloise's pastimes were pointed and intentional. She knew better than to question his intentions when it came to the safety of the house and those who resided within. He had risked his life more than once for them and would continue to do so. There was no need to prove his intentions each time he stepped out the door.

Eloise bit her lip and looked away, huffing in frustration.

"You said you almost died," she said, her tone softer. She refused to look at him and had her hands on her hips.

"Not for the first time," he reminded her.

"But you were on the other side of the world. You were gone, and we didn't know if you'd ever come back. What if you hadn't? What happens then?"

She finally looked at him again, the anger in her expression softened by a degree of visible fear and worry. If she were still alive, Shane was certain she would be on the brink of tears.

"But I came home. There's no point focusing on what didn't happen."

"Stop being so thick," she snapped. "Everyone survives until they don't. How dare you talk to me about not focusing on what didn't happen? I came to this house for a visit! For cakes and sandwiches and tea with my mother! I was supposed to survive that. You can't know when your time is coming, and you know it. You know it better than anyone, Shane Ryan."

"So, I should stay here forever?" Shane asked. "Be stuck in this house for the rest of my life?"

Eloise glowered, and her expression grew grim.

"No, of course not. I can't imagine what a nightmare it would be to find yourself stuck in this house forever."

She left without another word, and Shane sighed. He hadn't meant it in the way she'd taken it, but he realized he'd put his foot in his mouth. Eloise had been stuck in the house for more than a century, and she had a better perspective on what being rooted in one place forever meant.

She was angry now, and he would have to give her time to cool down. Regardless of misspoken words and unintentional insults, he couldn't ignore the threat the Reapers posed. He would have to solve that problem whether Eloise liked it or not.

As Eloise was so fond of pointing out, she might have looked like a little girl, but she was not. She understood why he had to leave even if she didn't want to admit it. Maybe he would speak with Carl about how to get her to be more realistic with her expectations.

Shane's plan for the day involved getting in touch with people he hadn't spoken to in many years. His life as a Marine was behind him, and he had not been looking to re-walk that path. But he would need to get in touch with some people if he wanted to find out what had become of Hawkins. Someone had to know.

One thing he knew for certain was that when it came to dealing with uncomfortable subjects, a face-to-face meeting was always better. People felt much more at ease lying over the phone than they did looking in someone's eyes. Especially if that someone was Shane.

"I won't ask how long you plan to be gone this time," Carl said as Shane got ready. Herbert and the Davis sisters had joined him to see Shane off. Eloise and Thaddeus were conspicuously absent.

"Shouldn't be as bad this time. I don't plan to get on any planes," he said.

"You should still take us with you," Dora told him.

"As a contingency plan," Daphne added.

"No one will even know we're there," Daisy said.

"Save it for watching the house," Shane said. "I doubt anyone will make a move again, but if they do, don't hesitate. They know ghosts, and they might have some weapons to help them next time."

"We will defend the house," Carl said. Shane knew anyone who entered was as good as dead. Everyone had been on edge since his return. Being away seemed to have pushed the spirits of the house closer to their more feral selves than he would have guessed, but their loyalty did not seem to waver.

He left without seeing Eloise. Lance Corporal Payton Halliday had been in Boston for a year or two and was one of the few Marines Shane had seen since he retired. He wouldn't call the man a friend, but they had served together briefly under Hawkins, and Halliday knew the man better. It was a place to start,

Shane smoked and drove and reached Boston fairly quickly thanks to light traffic. He was able to track down Halliday's home address and was at his door before lunch.

"Ryan?" Halliday said, opening his front door.

The other man was about Shane's height, with darker skin and a shaved bald head. He wore thick-rimmed glasses and looked a lot older and more tired than when Shane had last seen him.

"Good to see you, Corporal," Shane replied.

Halliday extended his hand and pulled Shane in for a hug, clapping him on the back with his free hand while he laughed. Shane accepted the overly familiar gesture and found himself oddly happy to see the other man. Memories of their time in Afghanistan flooded back, and it was like no time had passed.

"How the hell have you been?" Halliday asked, inviting Shane in.

"Alive, mostly," he replied.

"Barely, from the looks of you. You prize fight for a living now or something?" the other man chided.

"Something," Shane grinned.

Halliday offered Shane a seat at a dining room table then quickly went to the kitchen.

"You want coffee? Beer?" he asked.

"I'm good," Shane replied. Halliday got himself a beer and sat opposite Shane.

"What the hell, man? What are you doing here? What's been going on?"

"Got a problem I'm hoping you can help with. I need to find Captain Hawkins."

Halliday took a long pull of his beer.

"Hawkins? The CO? Man, that's a name I haven't heard in a while. Got dishonorably discharged, you heard that?"

"No," Shane answered. He wasn't surprised.

"I heard he got some soldiers killed. Bad intel, bad operation, a real mess. That was in Syria a few years back. Last I heard of the man. What do you need him for?"

"He's still getting people killed."

Halliday took another sip of beer.

"How's that?"

"He's in 'consulting' now. Military contractor. Runs a mercenary outfit in Europe, the Middle East. Probably everywhere else, too. Got Davis Blakely killed."

"Jesus," Halliday said softly. "Blakely's dead?"

"He's not the only one. You have any leads on where I can find him?"

Halliday shook his head.

"Like I said, man, he dropped off. Haven't even thought of him since back in the day. But if he's running some merc team, shouldn't you be calling the MPs or the CIA or something?"

"His men tried to kill me when I went to find out about Blakely. More than once. I'd kind of like to talk to him face to face," Shane replied.

"Not gonna lie, Ryan, that sounded cold," Halliday said with a laugh. "You look like the boogeyman, you know that, right?"

Shane had to laugh, but he shook his head.

"I just need to find him. What about Gonzalez or Tran or Hobbes? You got a line on any of them? I know they all retired on the East Coast somewhere."

"Hobbes is in Hartford; I know that for sure. Gonzalez is outside Portland somewhere. No idea about Tran. Oh, Patton! He's just down in Providence. He's probably your best bet, honestly."

"Alex Patton?" Shane asked. He vaguely remembered the man as being objectionable.

"That's Lieutenant Alexander Patton, thank you. That jackass was the XO. I guess that was after you retired."

"Yeah, that definitely was," Shane said. "Hawkins made him XO?"

"I think his dad, Major Patton, made him XO, but tomato, tomahto, you know?"

"Got it," Shane said.

If Hawkins stuck to his habit of trying to keep people he knew close, then maybe he was still in contact with his XO. Even if Patton wasn't part of Reaper Company, he would likely have some more up-to-date information on where Shane could find Hawkins. He would just have to play it carefully, in case the two were still working together.

"Providence, huh?" Shane asked.

"Yeah. He owns a private security company. Bodyguards and stuff."

"In Providence?" Shane asked. It didn't seem like the location for prime bodyguard work.

"Offices all over, man. LA, Miami, New York, Chicago. He's big time. Even more obnoxious than ever."

Shane thanked Halliday for his time and got up from the table, shaking the man's hand. If he hadn't been in such a hurry, he might have stuck around to share a beer and talk for a bit. Even though they hadn't been friends before, there was something about the camaraderie of being back with someone you served with that struck a chord with Shane.

Halliday gave him the name of Patton's company in Providence, and Shane got back on the road. He arrived in the city two hours later and then drove another fifteen minutes to find the address.

✳ ✳ ✳

Patton's company, Ironclad Security Services, operated out of an office that looked far too much like where the Reapers were in Vakovia.

The office was full of mirrored glass surfaces and sleek lines that made it look like something from the future. The exterior had a half-dozen visible security cameras, and there were at least twenty cars in the parking lot. Patton was doing pretty well for himself from the looks of things.

"Welcome to Ironclad Security Services. How can I help you?" a young, blonde woman at the reception desk asked when Shane entered. The place smelled like sandalwood and leather, and the furniture inside the lobby was black and modern. There was a small fridge with complimentary bottles of Voss water next to the reception area. Shane disliked it immediately.

"Need to see Alex Patton, please," he said.

"It's Mr. *Alexander* Patton," the woman corrected. "Do you have an appointment?"

"I don't. Tell him Shane Ryan is here. We served together under Captain Brett Hawkins."

"If you don't have an appointment, I can see if another consultant is free to help you, or you can leave your information, and Mr. Patton will get back to you at his earliest convenience."

Shane stared at the woman, who smiled thinly. He leaned on the desk and nodded toward her phone.

"I bet if you call him up right now and tell him Shane Ryan is here, and that we served together under Captain Hawkins, he's going to miraculously find a few minutes in his busy schedule to see me."

"Sir—" the receptionist began.

"Ma'am," Shane interrupted. "You work with Patton these days, so you know him better than me, I'm sure. If I'm right, and if he would have wanted to see me right now, how do you think he'll feel if he finds out you sent me on my way instead of just calling him to check?"

The receptionist's resolve cracked, though she retained a frosty demeanor.

"Please have a seat," she said before picking up the phone.

Shane opted to remain standing and waited. The receptionist spoke softly and then hung up the phone. She cleared her throat and took a sip of Voss.

"Mr. Patton will see you now. You can take the elevator to the fourth floor," she said.

"Thanks so much," Shane replied.

CHAPTER 3
BROKEN CHAINS

"Shane Ryan. There's a face I never thought I'd see again!"

Alexander Patton was loud and boisterous. He was not much taller than Shane, but he was a much wider and bigger man. He probably had at least fifty pounds of muscle on Shane, and since they had last seen each other, he had only bulked up.

In their limited time together, Shane had clocked Patton as a bully and an opportunist. He was the kind of soldier who liked to be the center of attention, and he liked to be right, no matter what. He had a cruel streak in him that seemed to bubble just under the surface. Getting into the private security business seemed right up his alley. Anything that permitted him to carry a gun and potentially hurt people.

"Patton. How have you been?" Shane said, keeping things cordial.

Patton's office looked to be the entire fourth floor. Lots of glass, lots of polished metal, and lots of toys. He had shooting games plastered on one wall like he owned an arcade and several display cases filled with firearms spanning from the present back to some Civil War-era muskets.

Shane could see no sign of any ghost, but if Patton was a Reaper, he might have been smart enough to hide it.

"Good. Great, even. Business is awesome, as you can see. Practically printing money, hanging out with celebrities, living the life, you know? What about you? Haven't seen you since... hell, I don't even know. You look like chopped meat!"

He laughed and clapped Shane on the shoulder, guiding him toward a glossy, black desk on the far side of the office.

IAN FORTEY AND RON RIPLEY

IAN FORTEY AND RON RIPLEY

"Scotch?" he asked, pouring two glasses before Shane could answer.

"Oh, you know. I keep busy these days," he said.

Patton laughed and set a glass in front of Shane before they sat.

"Busy? Hell, I read the news. You got sent up for trying to kill some politician in… what was it, Slovakia? Armenia?"

"Vakovia. Falsely accused and exonerated," Shane said. "That's actually why I'm here."

"Oh?" Patton replied, taking his scotch in a single gulp.

"I need to find Captain Hawkins. You have any contact?"

"Oh, wow. Hawkins? I am sorry, brother, but Hawkins went off the grid way back. He got a dishonorable and sort of faded into the night, you know what I'm saying?"

Patton would not stop smiling, and Shane found it aggravating. It was not a genuine smile, and his friendly tone was in stark contrast to the reality that they had never been friends and did not particularly like one another.

"You know anything about Reaper Company?" Shane asked. He didn't want to play coy with Patton. He wanted to see the man's reaction.

"What the hell is a Reaper Company?" he replied.

Was there something there? A little tightness at the eyes. The barest hint of tense neck muscles when he asked the question? It was impossible to tell.

"Mercenary team. Formally known as Silvershore Consulting. I hear Hawkins runs it. They're into some shady stuff. They're the ones behind the assassination attempt in Vakovia."

"No kidding?" Patton said. "I mean, I can't say I'm surprised. Hawkins wasn't above that kind of work, but what do I know? Like I said, he went off the grid ages ago. Maybe you can find something at the VA office."

"Yeah, maybe," Shane said.

Most mercenaries didn't register for veteran's benefits, and Patton knew that. He hadn't given Shane any specific reason not to trust him, but

Shane still didn't feel like he was getting honest answers. He just couldn't be sure if his brief history with the man and Patton's objectionable demeanor colored his opinion. Just because Patton was an asshole didn't technically make him a Reaper.

"Any other ideas on who might have stayed in touch?" Shane asked as he stood.

Patton grabbed the scotch from in front of Shane and took a drink, shrugging.

"Not my monkey, not my circus, these days," he answered. "Maybe try some of the other guys from the unit."

"Yeah. Maybe I'll do that." Shane said.

Patton led him back to the elevator, pointing out the various guns in his trophy cases and boasting about how much each cost. Shane said nothing and let the man gush about his collection.

"Listen, Ryan, whether you find Hawkins or not, feel free to give me a call if you're interested in some work. You'd be worth double any guy on my roster with that face of yours."

He laughed, and Shane smiled. Patton was ignorant, and a jerk, but he wasn't completely obtuse. He was baiting Shane now. That was the Patton Shane remembered. A guy who had to get in his digs at the expense of others just because he could.

"I'll keep that in mind," Shane said, entering the elevator.

Patton was already turning his back and walking away before Shane pressed the button for the first floor. He wasn't sure he trusted the man. Patton had never done anything to deserve Shane's trust, but he didn't seem like he was hiding murderous intent, either. For now, he was a dead end.

Hartford was only about an hour and a half from Providence. Corporal Jamie Hobbes was someone Shane had at least been friendly with back in Afghanistan. Hobbes stayed there longer than Shane and would have had more experience with Hawkins. He couldn't say for sure how long the relationship had been, but he was the next-best lead on the list.

Shane left the office, ignoring the cold glare from the receptionist on his way out. He was halfway to his car when he stopped to look back at the building. The mirrored glass windows didn't let him see anything inside, but he had a distinct feeling that someone was watching him.

It had been some years since Shane had visited Hartford. Tracking down Jamie Hobbes proved to take more time than the drive to the city had.

When the typical means of finding someone proved unhelpful, Shane headed to the VFW. There was a good chance the men inside would have known Hobbes if he showed up there, but they had no reason to share information with Shane, even if he was a fellow Marine. He was a stranger asking questions, and that would not be well received. That didn't mean no one at the VFW could give him information.

Outside the hall, just a stone's throw from the door, he found what he was looking for. What looked like a middle-aged man was skulking about in the shadows, his head down, and his hair a mess. No one on the street paid him a second glance because no one who passed by on the street could see him.

"You post up around here regularly?" Shane asked, approaching the ghost.

The spirit raised his head and sized up Shane with cloudy eyes set deep in a bruised face.

"Who's asking?"

"Just someone looking for an old friend. Marine corporal named Jamie Hobbes. Shorter than me, black hair, big nose. Likes to play cards," Shane replied.

"Sergeant," the ghost said. "He's a sergeant."

"How about that? So you know him," Shane said.

"I know everyone. Ricky Trunks, Dan Welman, Alberto Salvator, Hank Quentin, Terry Banks, John—"

"Got it," Shane said. "You know the whole crew. What's got you so into what these old-timers are up to?"

The ghost narrowed his eyes. Shane was standing in the street talking to him, but no one paid him any mind. The advent of phone earpieces had made anyone talking to themselves in public seem far less crazy for years now, but the ghost still seemed put off by it.

"You're not in the crew?" the ghost replied, his voice a little lower as though someone might overhear.

Shane took a shot in the dark.

"Reapers? Maybe," he said.

The ghost grinned and nodded.

"I knew it! I knew you'd come back recruiting sometime. I'm ready, boss. I'm ready! You take me out of here, and I will be the best soldier you ever had; I swear it!"

His enthusiasm was a little over the top, and now he seemed eager to be heard and noticed. Shane knew Reapers recruited ghosts from all over, but he hadn't expected to find them loitering in the hopes of getting picked up.

"First things first, soldier. I need to find Hobbes. Can't recruit a new asset unless I got a warm body to attach it to, right?"

"Hobbes? I don't think he can see us, boss. He never looked at me once. Plus, he's really sketchy these days. Drunk or high or whatever. Real sketchy," the ghost replied, his enthusiasm waning in favor of a touch of suspicion.

"Most can't see spirits until they undergo the procedure. We keep that under wraps. Tell me where to find him, and you'll find out soon enough," Shane lied. He was essentially speaking gibberish, but the ghost seemed to eat it up.

"Kensington, boss. He lives on Kensington, in that big, brown building. You can see it from here."

The ghost pointed east, and Shane followed with his eyes to an apartment that towered over everything nearby.

"Good man," Shane said, turning away.

"Wait," the ghost said, catching up and grabbing Shane's arm. "I'm in if he's in, right? You can take me out of here? I need to get out of here, boss. I need to be out there. Out in the world, you know?"

"If I recruit him, you're in," Shane said.

The ghost squeezed his arm harder, the cold seeping into his skin.

"I gotta get out of here, boss," he said, his voice lowering and his jaw tensing.

Shane grabbed the ghost's wrist firmly and pulled his hand away. He held on even as the spirit pulled back.

"You'll get what you get unless you have something to say about it right now," Shane told him. The ghost backed down quickly, surprised by the threatening tone and Shane's ability to physically touch him.

"No, boss! I mean... I just wanted to make sure you heard me."

"Heard," Shane replied. He left the ghost and made his way to Hobbes' apartment, hoping he'd finally found something worthwhile.

If ghosts were loitering around his VFW outpost and knew about the Reapers, he had to be getting closer.

CHAPTER 4

BREADCRUMBS

Hobbes lived in a rundown apartment building that had too many floors and too little upkeep. The exterior siding was chocolate brown, and it looked like a dead tree rising from a concrete tomb.

There was graffiti on the outside, and a pile of cigarette butts had been stomped out near the front doors. Shane could see that the parking lot along the west side of the building was equally full of graffiti, and a handful of young men watched Shane with more interest than was necessary as he approached the front doors.

The small vestibule inside the door had a massive board full of names and numbers that could be used to buzz up to the desired apartment. Shane scanned it for close to two minutes before he found Hobbes' number. He buzzed and waited.

"What?" came a staticky voice over the intercom.

"Nice to hear from you too, Hobbes. It's Shane Ryan. I need to talk to you."

There was a long silence, and then the static returned.

"I dunno any Shane Ryan."

The intercom shut off and Shane buzzed up again.

"Listen, bro—" Hobbes began, his voice slightly slurred.

"Afghanistan. 15th MEU," Shane said, cutting him off.

"Oh, crap. What's your name?"

"It's Shane Ryan, Hobbes. Are you drunk right now?"

"Just... nothing. Come on up. Twelfth floor."

There was a buzz as the lock released. Shane pulled open the door and headed up in a slow, humid elevator.

Hobbes was waiting with his head peeking out of his apartment door as Shane got off the elevator. He waved Shane over and held the door for him as he went inside.

The apartment building smelled like damp carpet and a hundred meals being cooked at the same time. Hobbes had lost about thirty pounds since Shane had seen him last and was in bad need of a shave and a clean set of clothes.

"Ryan!" Hobbes said with genuine enthusiasm. He looked like he hadn't slept in days and was wearing an old tank top and shorts. His apartment was a mess, and it was quite clear he lived alone.

"You look like hell, Hobbes," Shane said, standing just inside the entrance. The other man directed him to the left, into a cluttered living room littered with bottles, cans, and old food packages. There was a paused video game on the wall-mounted TV, and the room smelled of fried food and pot smoke.

"Look who's talking," Hobbes shot back. He pulled some trash off a chair and offered it to Shane, even though a chair on the opposite side of the coffee table was perfectly clear with no mess around it, and then flopped down on the couch. "This is crazy, man. How long's it been?"

"A while," Shane replied. "I need your help finding Captain Hawkins."

Hobbes grunted and took a half-finished beer off the coffee table, drinking it back until it was empty.

"You don't want to find that asshole," Hobbes said.

Shane said nothing, staring at Hobbes instead.

"What?" he asked.

"Why'd you say that?"

Hobbes shrugged and reached for another leftover beer.

"Doesn't mean anything," he said.

Shane's eyes drifted across the room. He scanned through all the trash, the discarded and crushed cans, the pizza crusts, and plates smeared with petrified ketchup or barbecue sauce residue. It looked very much like Hobbes did not spend a lot of time entertaining.

"What's with the chair?" he asked.

Hobbes looked to his left at the other chair on the clean, uncluttered side of the room.

"What? It's a chair."

Shane glanced at the hallway from which he'd come. One pair of shoes was at the doorway.

"You live alone?" Shane asked.

"Of course. Almost got married once but, you know… life happens."

"Sure," Shane said. He pointed at the empty chair. "Who sits there?"

Hobbes finished his second stale beer and shrugged.

"No one, man. Anyone. It's for guests."

"It's clean. The only clean spot in this room. Whoever sits there doesn't eat or drink."

Hobbes scoffed, a lazy half-laugh, and shrugged.

"What are you talking about, man? And hey, what have you been up to? Been a long time."

"I don't have time for small talk, Jamie. Hawkins' men had Davis Blakely killed. He tried to get his guys to kill me, too. I think you know exactly what kind of op he's running because I think you have a friend stashed in the back of this dumpster of an apartment who doesn't need to eat or drink."

Hobbes stared at him, and after a moment, barked a half-assed laugh and shook his head.

"Whatever you're on, man, let me try some."

Shane stood up and left the room, walking down the hall past the kitchen toward the single bedroom.

"Hey! Hey, what are you doing, man?" Hobbes called after him.

Shane pushed the bedroom door in as the other man rushed to catch up. He stopped as Shane stopped, staring into a clean, orderly space.

The walls were painted a soft yellow and decorated with framed photos. The bed was neatly made and matched the rest of the room. The curtains were drawn, but they were sheer and thin and still allowed the room to fill with sunlight, creating an almost hazy effect.

A woman sat at the foot of the bed, braiding her hair in front of a mirror that did not cast her reflection. She moved with slow, purposeful gestures and didn't make a sound.

"Man!" Hobbes said, turning away as he tossed up his hands in frustration. The woman did not stop braiding her hair. Pale fingers weaved in and out, creating the pattern as she worked her way to the base of the braid.

"Jamie, who is this?" she asked without turning her head. Her voice was soft and distant.

Shane could see bruises and needle marks along the woman's arms as she worked. They looked angry against the pale white of her dead flesh. He had seen similar markings on overdose victims.

"He's an old friend, babe. He just stormed in here!"

The ghost turned to look at Shane. Her eyes were milky, and her nose was caked with blackened blood. The flesh around her teeth had receded, making them look larger than they should have, and her lips were dry and flaky with bits of white crusted at the corners.

"Nosy, I see."

"Just trying to get some answers," Shane said. "You wouldn't happen to know Captain Hawkins, would you?"

"You said that was over," the ghost said to Hobbes, ignoring Shane. Her voice got louder, more demanding. "You said he was going to leave us alone."

"It is over! Ryan's just looking for him, and I told him I don't know where he is."

"You never said that," Shane said. "And I obviously don't believe you."

The ghost stood. Shane could see from the photos on the wall that she and Hobbes had been together once. Both looked much healthier and younger in the pictures. His almost bride, Shane guessed. Until the overdose.

"Get him out of here," the ghost ordered.

"Tell me how to find Hawkins, and I'm gone," Shane countered.

The ghost stormed toward him and raised a hand. Shane caught her by the wrist before she could slap him. She gasped in surprise, and Shane yanked her to one side so he could keep her and Hobbes where he could see them.

"What the hell is this?" Hobbes asked.

"This is me politely asking, for the last time, where I can find Hawkins, and what you know," Shane said.

The ghost moved to pull her arm away but Shane held fast, giving her a shake.

"I didn't come here to cause trouble. We used to be decent enough friends, if you can remember any of that. I don't care about her, or what you're doing now. I just need Hawkins."

"Jesus, Jamie, just tell him," the ghost said, making a face as she twisted her arm free. Shane let go suddenly, causing her to fall back.

The ghost fell through Jamie's legs, and he backed away with a shudder. Unlike Shane, he could not physically touch the spirit, but he could feel the cold as she passed through his body.

She got to her feet, scowling at Shane, and Hobbes finally relented.

"Listen, man, it's not like I know the guy, you know? Not really. He was our CO. He wasn't a guy I ever wanted to hang out with. He was a dick."

"But you saw him again," Shane said. "You reconnected Stateside."

"He came for me," Hobbes clarified. "I don't know how he knew, but he knew about Melissa."

Hobbes gestured to the ghost, and her foul mood seemed to subside. "Your girlfriend?" Shane asked.

"Fiancée," Melissa said. "We never made it to our wedding day."

"But she came back, and you can see her, so you get it. There are things in this world that most people don't know, you know?" Hobbes said, still trying to be coy.

"I know," Shane agreed.

"Well, so did Hawkins. I never found out how he knew, but he was looking to recruit me for a job. He needed guys like me. Like… us."

"He wanted people who could see the dead."

"*Soldiers* who could see the dead," Hobbes corrected. "He wanted a whole company of living and ghosts paired up to be an elite squad and do out-of-country missions for big paydays."

"Mercenaries," Shane said.

"Mercenaries," Hobbes repeated. "But I was done, man. I was… I mean, I smoke some weed now, but back then, I was into it. I was strung out. I lost my fiancée, I was out of the Marines, I had nothing going, and…"

"I get it," Shane said.

"I couldn't do it even if I wanted to. And I didn't! I swear I didn't want it. Hawkins was really pissed, acting like I owed him something and blew it. He got angry, Ryan. Like really angry."

"What do you mean?"

"I ended up moving. Laying low for a long while. Pretending I couldn't see that old ghost out at the VFW or any of them, just so no one thinks I'm part of this thing. I thought he was going to have someone come back and off me. Like he realized he told me too much before I agreed to anything, and he had to fix it. He never did, but he told me to get cleaned up and then get back to him. He'd keep a spot for me."

"Did he leave you a way to contact him?" Shane asked.

"Not really. But, I mean, I was at his office, if you can call it that. More of a house. I know where he works," Hobbes replied.

"I need that address," Shane said.

Hobbes looked uncomfortable as he paced in the hallway next to his dead fiancée.

"Come on, Ryan. If you're planning something, and he finds out it was me—"

"I'd be more worried about me right now than Hawkins," Shane said. "Give me the address and I'll leave. Hawkins will never know I was here."

"It was years ago, man! He could have moved or—"

"Just give it to him, Jamie!" Melissa yelled, a wave of chilled air coming off of her.

Hobbes relented and wandered into the bedroom, opening a drawer, and rifling through a disorganized pile of papers beneath his socks.

Finally, he pulled out a card and handed it to Shane.

The card had the name Silvershore Consulting on it, and a Connecticut address.

"Thank you, Hobbes," Shane said, slipping the card into his pocket.

He slipped past the man and the ghost and made for the apartment door.

"Ryan, man, what are you doing? You remember Hawkins, right? He's way worse now than he was back then. He's a dangerous guy."

"So am I," Shane said before leaving.

CHAPTER 5
SILVERSHORE

The address on the business card was not in Hartford as Shane expected. It wasn't in any city. Instead, it was listed as being somewhere just outside of Salmon River State Forest. Silvershore's headquarters was just a rural address, nothing like where a military contracting firm should have been located.

Shane drove out of Hartford cautiously. If Hawkins was working out on the sticks, there was a reason for it. Obviously, he was going to have increased privacy, but the nature of his work didn't mesh with the location. It was immediately suspicious, and he needed to proceed accordingly.

The drive out of Hartford was only about a half-hour before he found himself on secluded, tree-lined roads, crossing bridges over little streams and babbling brooks.

Shane found the right street and proceeded slowly toward the address. He was in the beautiful, open countryside. It was the kind of place people retired after they were sick of spending their lives in cities. Lush, green trees, wide fields of wildflowers, birds singing, and sun shining. It was the opposite of everything Reaper Company seemed to be.

Ahead of him on the right, land rose slightly to reveal a large country home set into a lawn that must have taken hours to mow. There were neatly trimmed hedges, expertly landscaped flower beds, and a long, paved driveway that led out to the road. The mailbox out front had the correct address plastered on the side of it.

Shane drove by without slowing the vehicle so as not to seem suspicious to anyone in the house who might have been looking out. He passed by, seeing no one, and only observing a single car parked out front. Nothing about it met his expectations. It was a house, not a business. It looked like the family home of someone's grandparents. The only obscure feature was a helipad a short distance from the house, beyond the driveway.

He found the nearest side street and pulled over at the first opportunity to hide his car. Instead of following the road back, he cut across the untamed forest and made his way around to the rear of the house, hiding beyond the enormous, perfect lawn and sticking to the distant trees of the nearby woods.

Directly behind the house, he posted up behind some trees and shrubs where he felt that he would be out of sight. From this new vantage point, he could see people on the property, they just weren't alive.

A handful of ghosts were on the grounds, a pair walking and talking while another sat on a bench near a small koi pond. A fourth leaned against the house, and a fifth was standing and staring at nothing Shane could see.

Shane stayed hidden and watched as the walking ghosts went around the house and several others appeared. Although they were casual and seemed to be in no rush, the pattern of movement struck him as a security patrol. Hardly intense and well-regulated, it was still clear that several ghosts were circling the building while others were in stationary positions.

Security cameras were placed around the house's exterior. They hung from eaves and corners, and the spread was thorough enough that Shane doubted there was an inch that wasn't being covered. He could see at least six cameras on the back wall, and more along the sides. The front would probably be the same.

Ghosts came and went from the house. During the next hour, he saw at least ten spirits on the property. Even if it looked like a country home, the number of dead indicated something else was going on. Shane just couldn't understand why Hawkins had chosen to operate undercover rather than have a business like Silvershore did outside the country.

The night was closing in when Shane decided to reposition and watch the house from the front. He skirted the property, keeping low, with his eyes on the ghost guards until he was close to the road on which he had passed the house earlier in the day.

Posting up in the weeds and underbrush, Shane finally caught sight of a living person coming out of the house just before sunset. Even at a distance, after several years, he recognized Captain Hawkins.

Hawkins was dressed in a suit and wore sunglasses despite the late hour. There was still something arrogant about the way he carried himself, but different from what Shane remembered. Out of the military, he had become a different sort of person.

The man went to the vehicle parked outside and took a small box out of the trunk. He returned to the house with it, and Shane continued watching until the sun had completely set.

The pattern of the ghost patrols around the house had not changed. Shane waited until a predictable break arose, one that would give him about five minutes to get to the front door, and left his hiding place.

He used trees and some of the landscape to keep out of sight as best as he could. His hope was that, in the darkness, without the ghost guards catching sight of him, no one would notice anything.

Shane reached the front door and considered knocking. Before he did, he tried the handle and found it unlocked. The door pushed in easily and silently, and he stood on the porch for only a moment before ducking inside.

Something felt off. To have the dead as security guards, to have a full spread of cameras, and then to leave your door unlocked did not make sense. Neither did it make sense to run a mercenary outfit out of a country home in Connecticut.

Shane closed the door behind him and entered the house. The interior matched the exterior perfectly. A large living room to the left of the door was full of sofas, high ceilings with a skylight, and a massive TV on one wall.

Framed photographs decorated the walls and end tables. Shane could see photos of Hawkins with his family: his wife and children, and others depicting just the kids, including a son in a baseball uniform. This was a family home. If it was a disguise, it was well done.

Of course, if Hawkins was trying to keep Reaper Company a secret, then he didn't need to hide the ghosts. Most people would never see them. That's why they walked freely as guards around the property. The house kept up appearances for normal people, not people like Shane. Not people like the members of Reaper Company.

If someone doubted that Hawkins was running a legitimate business, they could come to the house and see that it was just his quaint family home. He probably had an office somewhere in the house with a big desk and a computer. Nothing that looked out of place or dangerous if the military wanted to ask questions. But there was something somewhere. The ghosts were not there to guard a laptop.

Shane stood just inside the door and listened to the house. He could hear the hum of various electronics in the background, an air conditioner running somewhere, but little else. There were no voices, no one was watching television, and it didn't sound like anyone was moving about.

The ghost guards were nowhere to be found on the inside of the house. He looked over the living room and saw no indication of spirits or Hawkins, or that anyone had been in the room recently.

Shane proceeded deeper into the house. He walked as carefully as he could, ensuring he made as little sound as possible. Every few steps he would stop again to listen, but there was nothing new for him to hear.

He ducked into several rooms and looked around, finding nothing in the bathroom, a small study, or the kitchen. The dining room and a pantry were equally empty of people or spirits.

There was a bowl of fruit in the kitchen, the cupboards were stocked, and the pantry looked like it had been recently filled as well. Everything looked natural, not staged or faked for anyone trying to investigate. Shane had every reason to believe this was Hawkins' real house.

A floorboard creaked.

Shane froze in place in the kitchen, holding his breath. A soft thud above his head caused him to look up. Someone was on the second floor.

He moved to the stairs, quickly but silently, and waited at the base with his neck craned to see up. The stairs curved right, preventing him from seeing the top. There was a light up there but no shadows or movement he could see.

Carefully, Shane took the first few steps. He reached the landing that curved to the next flight and paused, sticking his head around the corner to look up and listen again. No more sounds and no movement waited for him.

Shane ascended the stairs one step at a time. Three steps from the top, the wood of the stair creaked underfoot. It was a thin, swift whine, and Shane froze. Though it was quick, the sound was sharp and loud. Anyone within earshot would have heard it and known immediately what it was.

No one called out or came rushing to see who was there. No ghost guard attacked him. Nothing happened.

Shane waited again at the top of the stairs, hoping for some sign of what waited for him. He was on edge. Part of him was eager to track down Hawkins, but part of him suspected something else was happening. Had Hawkins not heard him on the step? And where were the ghost guards?

A faint noise broke the silence. The sound of a drawer closing, or someone setting something down; it was hard to say. But it came from the left at the end of the hall.

Shane made his way toward the noise. The hallway carpet muffled his footsteps, and he moved as silently as a ghost. He reached the door at which he'd heard the sound and took the knob in his hand. It was room temperature, no indication that a ghost waited on the other side.

The door opened smoothly and silently. Shane had opened the door to Hawkins' office. A large, oak desk sat close to the far wall and faced the rest of the room. Behind it, in a highbacked office chair, sat Alexander Patton.

"Shane Ryan. What are the odds of that?" Patton said with a grin. He took a sip from a glass tumbler.

"Patton? What the hell are you doing here?"

"Just waiting for you. I wanted to watch."

The thunder of footsteps racing up the stairs behind him caused Shane to turn away from the door. Armed men in black tactical vests spilled into the hallway. Patches identified them as FBI. Three men trained automatic rifles on Shane as Hawkins made his way between them to the head of the group.

"That's him," Hawkins said.

The lead FBI agent approached Shane with a sidearm drawn and aimed between Shane's eyes.

"Turn around," the man said, using one hand to pull handcuffs from his belt. Shane's eyes were locked on Hawkins. His former CO smiled but said nothing.

The agent pushed Shane back harshly as a second one held him against the wall and flipped him around. They handcuffed him as they shouted commands that Shane was not necessarily resisting but barely listening to, either.

Hawkins opened the next door in the hallway. Huddled together inside were his wife and what must have been his grandchildren.

"It's okay; it's all over. They caught him," Hawkins said, comforting the young ones. Another FBI agent entered the room with them, and soon, everyone was talking over everyone else as Shane was shoved out of the way.

His hands were cuffed behind his back, and he stumbled as he was pushed toward the stairs. Patton was talking to one agent and Hawkins to another. They were taking statements from the children. Shane heard talk of threats and stalking as an agent led him down the stairs and out the front of the house.

A dozen vehicles waited out front, most unmarked, but several with lights flashing. More agents and local police were there, all watching as Shane was led to a black sedan and pushed into the rear seat.

"You have the right to remain silent," began the agent who put Shane into the car. "Anything you choose to say could be used against you in a court of law."

Shane stared out the windshield, the rest of the script buzzing in his ear like white noise.

The ghost guards stood outside, watching Shane Ryan get arrested. Most of them were smiling.

CHAPTER 6

DARK DAYS

"Making terroristic threats. Stalking. Murder. Kidnapping. Theft. Arson. Destruction of property. Treason. Jesus Christ, is there anything you haven't been accused of?"

The FBI agent's name was Betts. Shane hadn't caught a first name, not that he cared. Betts had rattled off a list of everything Shane was accused of doing in Vakovia with a few new charges tossed in related to Hawkins and his family. Stalking, terroristic threats, and harassment. He had no idea what evidence there was to support that, but he didn't doubt that Hawkins had produced something.

"You'll notice that all that was dropped," Shane pointed out.

"Not all of it," Betts said. "Stalking. Breaking and entering. Threats. We got you dead to rights on those, Ryan."

"I'm sure you think you do," he replied.

He was in a very small room, in a very uncomfortable chair, handcuffed to a metal table, and facing a large mirror. A TV was mounted on the wall at his left. He was certain there were agents on the other side of the mirror. Maybe a district attorney as well.

"Is there another reason why you were at Mr. Hawkins' home?" Betts asked.

"Just wanted to talk to the man," Shane answered.

"Never heard of a telephone?"

"Didn't have his number."

Betts smiled and shrugged.

"You don't have to work with me, but you have to know you're in too deep here, Ryan. The Vakovian government might have dropped charges against you, but we have access to security footage from at least six locations. We've got you blowing up a helicopter."

"Do you, though?" Shane asked.

He had been present for more than one helicopter explosion, actually, but none of his direct actions had caused them to explode. Certainly nothing that would have shown up on camera.

"Maybe," Betts said. "Or maybe it wasn't you. Maybe it was ghosts, huh?"

Shane didn't react, but the question caught him off-guard. Betts glanced at the mirror, and a moment later, the door to the room opened. A tall man in a gray suit entered, his hair even grayer than his jacket, and he shook hands with Betts.

"Doctor," the agent said.

"Agent Betts."

The doctor sat down opposite Shane, setting a briefcase down on the table to his left, and smiled.

"Hello, Mr. Ryan. My name is Dr. Loomis. May I call you Shane?"

Shane didn't reply. Dr. Loomis was up to no good; Shane had no doubt about that.

"Shane, I'd like to ask you some questions, and I hope you'll answer them honestly. I want to help you with this situation you're in, and I want you to know that, at any time, you can ask for an attorney to be present. Do you understand?"

"Sure," Shane replied.

"Great. Before we start, is there anything I can get you? Coffee, a soda?"

"Could really use a smoke about now."

"You can't smoke in government buildings," Betts told him.

"Is that another charge?" Shane asked. "Terroristic combustion?"

"Shane," Dr. Loomis said, drawing his attention back. "I want to ask you about your recent trip to Vakovia. You went there to see a friend, a Marine you once served with, is that correct?"

"Seems like you know the answer to that."

"But this friend had died in Vakovia. Why did you go if you knew he was dead?"

"Heard the weather was nice there. Hot, but dry."

Dr. Loomis ignored the response and continued to ask Shane about Blakely, Silvershore, the explosion at the Silvershore headquarters, and the fire at the ironworks. Shane either ignored the questions or redirected them.

"Shane, tell me about ghosts."

He looked blankly at Dr. Loomis. Both the doctor and Betts were watching him now.

"Isn't it true you talk to ghosts? And you believed your friend Blakely was working with them?"

"We almost done here?" Shane replied.

"If you think you're getting a break from this now or ever, you got another thing coming," Betts told him.

"Tell me about your house, Shane. Do you believe it's haunted? That you live there with spirits you've befriended?"

Shane sighed and tried to lean back, but the cuffs prevented him.

"So, this is it?" he said. "Going to try to paint me as a lunatic? Guy who talks to ghosts or something? Have me committed? Based on what?"

"Shane, I want you to look at something for me," Dr. Loomis said.

He pulled a remote control from his briefcase and used it to turn on the TV. The image that appeared was of Shane inside a vehicle. He didn't recognize it.

Dr. Loomis pressed play, and the shaky footage started. It looked like some kind of dashboard camera facing into a vehicle from just above the steering wheel. Shane was driving alone, but it was not his car.

"Does it look like I like this?" Shane said in the video, with the car moving erratically. "Where to now?"

The background noise was squealing tires and honking horns. Shane jerked the wheel left and right and swayed in the seat with his sudden turns.

"Then where?" he said.

"We go off the bridge?"

"Trust you?" he said a moment after.

The video played until the moment the car crashed and went into a river. Shane remembered it all quite well. He had stolen the car from behind a shop in Vakovia. Reapers and local police were chasing him. Oleg the Brute and Radek Dorn were his passengers. Neither spirit showed up on camera, nor did any of the things they'd said been heard.

"You drove this car off the Yesenk Bridge and into a river, do you remember that?" Dr. Loomis asked, pausing the video.

"Rings a bell," Shane admitted.

"Can you tell me who you were talking to in the video? It seems like you were having a very intense conversation, and that someone instructed you to drive that car into the river. Is that what happened?"

Shane let out a long sigh. He'd seen that camera on the dash when he got into the car, he just hadn't thought anything of it. He had had more important things on his mind at the time.

"Can't a man talk to himself in the car anymore?" Shane replied.

Dr. Loomis smiled sympathetically.

"I know how real this all must seem to you, Shane. And I know how hard it is to have that perception challenged. I'm a stranger; you have no reason to trust me. But I want you to know that I am here to help you. I'm not with the FBI. I'm a doctor, and my only concern is helping you get better."

Dr. Loomis didn't speak in a condescending or patronizing tone. The fact that his words rang with genuine sympathy and sincerity made something in Shane's stomach twist. He was selling this narrative, and he was selling it very well.

Shane's back was against the wall, and his options had been taken from him. There were two paths ahead: He could try to fight his way out of that room and get shot in the process, or he could accept that Hawkins had set this up and, for the time being, had won.

"Aren't I the lucky guy?" Shane said dryly.

"You drove that car off a bridge and into a river, Shane. You were having an active conversation with people who weren't there, and it looks to me like they convinced you to do this. Do you think that is something a healthy person would have done? Be honest."

Shane grunted and said nothing. Dr. Loomis turned to Betts and stood.

"I'd like to take him into my custody now."

"Whatever you say, Doc," Betts agreed.

"Shane," Dr. Loomis said, turning back to face him. "I'm going to get you out of this place, okay? You're going to come back to the hospital where I work, and we're going to help you."

Shane couldn't help but laugh. The number of times he had to go to some kind of asylum or psychiatric hospital to track down a ghost was greater than he would like to admit. Never once on any of those visits had he thought he would end up in one of those places himself. He should have brought the Davis sisters with him. Maybe they could have shown him the ropes.

Another agent entered the room and released Shane from the cuffs on the table. He was quickly reshackled behind his back and led outside.

Betts and Dr. Loomis talked as Shane was being escorted behind them down hallways through whatever federal office building he was in. The doctor filled out some paperwork, and Shane stood around as though he didn't exist. It was like he had been bought at an auction and they were finalizing the transaction.

He was taken to an underground parking structure and loaded into the back of a small, windowless truck where, once again, he was handcuffed to a wall. The agent with him sat on a bench opposite him and said nothing.

"Don't worry, Shane. We'll get you into a room and make sure you're comfortable. Tomorrow, after a good night's rest, we can talk about a plan to help you move forward," Dr. Loomis said before closing the door.

The truck engine roared to life, and soon enough, they were on the road. Shane stared at the agent, who stared back at him.

"Hell of a gig you got here. You babysit everyone on the way to the nuthouse, or is this a special assignment?" he asked.

The agent didn't reply.

Shane guessed they had been on the road for the better part of an hour when the truck began to slow, and he could feel them take a sharp right. The truck proceeded at a much slower pace for another minute or so until it came to a stop. The agent with him had not spoken a word, nor had the scowl on his face changed much.

The rear door opened, and the agent uncuffed Shane. It was not Dr. Loomis releasing him this time but a pair of orderlies in hospital scrubs who swapped Shane's FBI handcuffs for a set of hospital restraints.

"Really going to miss you," Shane told the agent as the new men led him away.

It was too dark for Shane to see any signage in front of the building he was being led into. The hospital was large and foreboding. It looked like it had been built sometime around the Second World War. The architecture was severe, and he marveled, not for the first time, at how mental hospitals looked like they were specifically designed for ghosts to haunt.

He could already see one spirit outside of the building, a wizened-looking man in a dirty robe who was hunched over and ignoring the orderlies and Shane. They made their way to a pair of unusually tall, reinforced glass doors that marked the front entrance.

The inside of the hospital smelled like industrial cleansers. It was extremely antiseptic, almost to the point of being aggravating. One of the orderlies signed Shane in at the front desk where the night nurse barely glanced in his direction from behind a glass shield that ensured no patients or others could gain access to the door controls.

The night nurse buzzed the next set of doors, and Shane was led through and down a long corridor of identical, cream-colored doors. Each one featured a small window and a narrow slot along the floor to push food trays through. It looked like a prison.

Shane was led to a room marked 35B. One of the orderlies unlocked the door, and then he was led inside a small, square room that featured a twin bed, a wardrobe, and a small table with a chair. There was even a window, albeit heavily covered with bars to ensure no one would escape from it. The setup was actually nicer than he expected.

"Should I put in my breakfast order now or just call down when I wake up?" Shane asked.

He managed to get a laugh out of the orderly who unlocked his restraints, but it was the other man who answered him.

"Dr. Loomis will be back in the morning. There's a bathroom through the door on the left. You have a call button, which is only for emergencies. Abuse it, and we will disconnect it. Respect us, and we respect you. If you're disruptive, aggressive, or disorderly with us or the other patients, you can be confined to the room, restrained, or put into solitary until you calm down. Do you understand?"

"Loud and clear," Shane replied.

"Good. I'm Jacob, this is Arnold. Get some sleep, and we'll get you sorted in the morning."

Jacob and Arnold left the room, and a loud, heavy lock clicked into place. Shane sat on the small bed, the gesture sending up the smell of bleach from the linens.

This was going to be a serious problem.

Shane woke up to sunlight streaming between the bars of the window and hitting him in the face. Despite the conditions, he had managed to fall asleep. He earned nothing by staying awake all night, so he figured he might as well get some rest.

He sat up slowly and yawned, realizing for the first time that he was not going to be able to smoke a cigarette that morning. He had barely been back in the United States long enough to enjoy about a pack's worth, and he was right back to where he had been in Vakovia.

"This isn't your room."

The voice came from the bathroom door. Shane glanced over to the side of the room untouched by sunlight. A ghost hunched in the doorway, sitting on his haunches, with his feet holding the bathroom door frame. He looked like a frog.

The spirit was old, his face was wrinkled, and his jowls hung like a sad hunting dog. His eyes were damp as though he had just been crying, and his skin had a yellow cast.

"I asked for a suite, but this was all they had open," Shane said.

"You think you're funny," the ghost replied. Half of his body was hidden in the bathroom doorway. He looked like he was ready to duck back into the other room at a moment's notice.

"Comedy is subjective," Shane said.

"You won't laugh for long. Not in here. Not when they start with you."

The ghost grinned as though he'd made a joke. Shane swung his feet over the edge of the bed and stood.

"Meaning?" he asked.

"You'll see," the ghost answered.

Shane took a step toward the spirit, and he scuttled back into the bathroom. By the time Shane got to the doorway, the ghost had vanished.

There were no toiletries in the bathroom, so all Shane could do was wash his face with cold water. He returned to the bed and sat, waiting for what came next. It was at least two hours before the door was unlocked.

Dr. Loomis entered the room, wearing a white coat over his suit. A new orderly was with him, a larger man with a crewcut and thick-rimmed glasses. His arms strained the fabric of his uniform, and he looked more like a bodybuilder than anything else. Dr. Loomis smiled at Shane as he read a chart.

"Shane, how are you this morning?"

"Locked in a mental hospital, you?"

Dr. Loomis' smile didn't break.

"In good spirits, I see. I had a chance to go over your charts last night, Shane, and I want to start you on a course of zuclopenthixol. I think it's going to be the best medication for you right now, so I'm going to need you to roll up your sleeve for me."

Shane chuckled and shook his head.

"Seriously? You think I'm going to let you inject me with whatever the hell that is?"

The orderly took a step forward, but Dr. Loomis raised a hand to stop him.

"Shane, I'm trying to help you. We need to get your symptoms in check before we can hope to make progress. What do you say?"

Movement from the corner of his eye caught Shane's attention. The wrinkled, jowly ghost was watching from the bathroom doorway with an unreadable expression. Shane ignored him and focused on Dr. Loomis.

"Not happening," he said.

"Ephram, would you lend a hand, please," Dr. Loomis asked.

The big orderly came forward and Shane rose to meet him.

"Hands to yourself, Ephram," Shane said.

Without warning, the orderly threw a punch and clipped Shane in the jaw. The blow was powerful, and Shane's head snapped back as he fell back to the bed. Ephram wasted no time leaning over Shane and punching him in the face again and again before rolling him over harshly. The big orderly threw a leg up and got on the bed with him, straddling Shane's back and forcing his head into the pillow.

Shane could taste blood in his mouth, and he struggled to breathe as the larger man's hand forced him down, smothering him.

"Thank you, Ephram," Dr. Loomis said casually. Shane turned his head to the side so he could breathe, blood sputtering in his nose, and he watched the doctor check the level of liquid in a syringe.

"This is a fifty-milligram dose to start you off, with a mild dose of lorazepam and ketamine to keep you feeling calm. Tomorrow, we'll try switching you to pills if you seem like you'll be a little more cooperative."

Dr. Loomis stuck Shane in the arm with the needle and pushed the plunger. He nodded at Ephram, and the big orderly got off of Shane's back and let him go. For just a moment, Shane stayed where he was and then sat up again. The orderly punched him in the face again, and he collapsed back onto the bed.

"We'll come to see how you're doing in a few hours," Dr. Loomis said cheerfully before turning away.

They left the room and locked the door behind them. Shane sat up and raised a hand to his nose. It wasn't broken, but he was bleeding profusely.

He stumbled on his way to the bathroom, and the creeping ghost from the doorway vanished again when he got too close. The water stung as he washed his face, and his head began to swim as he cleaned himself up.

Shane wasn't sure what Dr. Loomis had injected him with, but it was taking effect. He made his way back to bed and focused on keeping his thoughts clear. Ten minutes had passed, and he began to feel drowsy even though he had just woken up. Another ten minutes, and he was barely able to sit up.

He slumped back onto the bed and felt a warm numbness radiating throughout his body. The ceiling above his head seemed to spin very slowly, pulsing in time with his heartbeat. Shane knew the drugs were taking effect, and he fought them. He focused on the light above him, trying to keep it straight and stationary in his head. But the more he tried, the more the world around the light seemed to twist and bend.

"Already got you beat," the bathroom ghost said, his voice sounding like it was coming through layers of padding.

Shane lifted his head to look for the spirit, but his neck muscles felt like jelly. He flopped from side to side and realized he could lift his hands but couldn't feel his arms. They fell to his side when he thought about how to sit up properly and couldn't hold on to the thought for more than a few seconds.

The ghost appeared at his bedside, still crouched low, grinning insidiously as he leaned forward to look Shane in the eyes.

"They got you so good now," the ghost said, giggling.

"No," Shane said.

His tongue felt like a foreign object. It was hard to make his lips work properly, and focusing on the meaning of words was difficult.

The ghost continued to laugh, and Shane found it impossible to focus on the spirit's face. Everything inside of him was heavy. Not crushingly heavy, but too heavy to lift. His body felt like it was unwinding, every little piece coming undone and set aside, and he was no longer a whole thing. Shane closed his eyes, and the world was swallowed up.

Sounds came to him now and then. He tried to speak, but sometimes couldn't remember what speaking was. Memories flashed through his mind of Vakovia, Afghanistan, and the house on Berkley Street.

The girl in the pond came to him. Her cruel laugh chased him through the darkness, and he fell into the cold, empty water.

He opened his eyes, and he was in a hospital room. A spirit with shockingly red hair leaned over him, her jaws wired shut and her eyes wild. He reached for her, but it was as though he no longer had arms. His eyes fell shut, and he was whisked away to another place and time.

Dreams and memories rolled together in a jumbled mess inside his head. He could no longer tell if he was experiencing things that had happened, or if someone was speaking in his ear describing people and events he could barely understand.

Part of his mind told him it wasn't real, but it was only a voice in the crowd. His voice was one of hundreds, and each one was as hard to identify as another.

The only real thought he could hold onto was how tired he was. How everything in his body was demanding he sleep. He wanted to keep his eyes closed, to lie in that bed and stay warm and comfortable forever. He couldn't conceive of a reason why he would ever want to do anything else.

Dr. Loomis appeared. He was speaking, but Shane couldn't make out the words. It was noise. It was an unformed sound, like the man had a mouthful of food and was just humming around it. Shane tried to respond but couldn't tell if he was speaking.

Shane blinked again, and it was dark. The room was empty. He struggled to keep his eyes open, willing himself to be awake. How much time had passed?

He rolled onto his side and stared at the big, cream-colored metal door. That was not his door. This was not his room. He was not in his house. He was in a hospital. He remembered that. He had been sent to a hospital by someone.

"Carl," he said, struggling to form the word.

No. Carl could not answer. Carl was home, and Shane was not home.

Shane's muscles felt like liquid. He wanted to sit up, but it was so hard.

He clenched his teeth and swore inside his head, trying to hold focus.

"Shhh…" he said, half-forming a curse. He struggled to make his arms and back and legs function as one. It took five minutes, maybe ten, but he sat up.

The ghost of a woman was at the foot of his bed. Red hair hung past her shoulders, some of it twisted into knots. Metal wires protruded from between her lips as though she had pulled them free from her jaws as they were being held shut.

"You won't last," the bathroom ghost whispered. He was behind the redheaded woman, still skulking in shadows.

"How long have I been…" Shane asked.

"All day. All day tomorrow. All day every day soon," the bathroom ghost giggled.

Shane felt dizzy and stayed in one spot for a long time, hoping the feeling would go away. It didn't.

Finally, slowly, he got to his feet.

"Bad idea," the bathroom ghost said in a singsong voice.

"Shut up," Shane mumbled. He straightened, stood next to the bed on shaky legs, and took a step. The world moved faster than he did, causing him to fall forward and land hard on the linoleum floor.

The bathroom ghost laughed until a clicking sound from outside the room silenced him.

"What?" Shane asked. He was face-down on the floor, enjoying the cool sensation of the tile. The click sounded again in the hall. It was far away but getting closer, sounding again every couple of seconds.

Click… click… click…

He turned his head, and the bathroom ghost was gone. The redhead had backed into the corner.

"What's happening?" Shane asked.

The ghost raised a finger to her wired mouth as though to shush him but made no sound. She took one more step into the shadows and vanished.

Click… click… click…

The sound from the hall grew closer but not faster. It sounded like someone was taking a leisurely stroll down the hallway and knocking against the doors as they went.

Click.

It was very close now, and Shane forced himself to sit up, looking up at the small window in his door.

Click.

The sound was right outside now. Something had hit his door. Darkness filled the small window, and something pushed gently at the small flap just above the floor through which food trays were passed.

Shane focused, but nothing distinct came through. The shadow moved away from the window, and he heard the sound again a moment later, farther away.

Click… click… click.

The sound continued down the hallway away from Shane until he no longer heard anything.

"What was—" he began to ask.

A scream cut through the night, muffled by distance but unmistakable. Shane crawled to the bathroom and got to his knees at the sink.

He needed to get his head clear.

CHAPTER 8
PLAYING THE GAME

"Shane."

Shane opened his eyes. He felt cold and weak. He was staring at a wall, and it was hard to pull his thoughts together.

"Shane, are you awake?"

He blinked to try to clear his eyes. Someone was standing over him. Slowly, he rolled his head to one side and looked up. He was on the floor, and Dr. Loomis was standing before him.

"It looks like you fell out of bed," the doctor said.

"Oh. Sure," Shane agreed. "Wild party last night."

Dr. Loomis smiled and someone else came from the doorway. Shane moved away, but he was still so weak and groggy. The orderly, Ephram, picked him off the ground under the arms and foisted him onto the bed.

"How are you feeling about things this morning?" Dr. Loomis asked.

"Drugged," he answered and then smiled. He knew his head was still fuzzy, but it was so hard to keep it focused on anything.

"Well, as we regulate your dosage, hopefully, things will even out for you until we can decide what needs to be done with you."

"What needs to be done with me?" he asked. Dr. Loomis chuckled.

"I imagine we'll have an answer to that sooner rather than later. But in the meantime, we don't want you hurting yourself or anyone else. Take this."

He held out a small paper cup with two tiny pills in it. Shane glanced from the doctor to the orderly and then to the cup. He knew he shouldn't take the pills, but if he resisted, there was a good chance his new friend

Ephram was going to make him regret it.

"Okay," he said.

He took the little cup and upended it into his mouth. Dr. Loomis handed him a second tiny cup full of water that Shane used to swallow the pills.

"Refreshing," he said, handing the cup back.

Ephram grabbed Shane's face in one hand and squeezed, forcing his mouth open. He jammed his fingers inside and rooted around, finding the pills under Shane's tongue.

With his other hand, Ephram grabbed hold of Shane's side along his ribs and squeezed the soft tissue. It felt like pliers pressing down on him, and he groaned in pain. The big man's forefinger pushed the pills to the back of Shane's throat and then forced Shane's mouth closed, covering his mouth and nose.

Shane struggled to breathe, the wet pills sticking to his tongue. He sputtered and eventually felt them slide down his throat. Ephram let him go.

"Please don't try that again, Shane. We'll have to go back to higher-dose injections if you do."

"Yeah," Shane said, breathing sharply. "Okay."

"I think we're going to have to keep you in your room until you get a feel for how things operate here, and I can be sure you're trustworthy."

Shane flopped back on the bed and zoned out the rest of what Dr. Loomis had to say. He stayed in the room for another two minutes or so before leaving and taking Ephram with him.

After listening for any more sounds of people in the halls, Shane sat up again.

"You're gonna die here," the bathroom ghost told him. Shane wondered if the spirit ever left the room or if he had been haunting that specific bathroom for years.

"Did you die in here?" Shane asked, getting to his feet.

He still felt unsteady, but he was surer on his feet than he had been the day before. Whatever he had been injected with was slowly wearing off. The pills, however, had yet to kick in, so he still had some time.

"Never died," the ghost said. "Never die."

"Okay," Shane replied.

He stumbled toward the bathroom, listing left and right and having to extend his arms to keep himself on track. The ghost scuttled away again before he got too close, and by the time he reached the bathroom, he had vanished.

Shane turned on the faucet and cupped his hand under it, slurping up a couple of mouthfuls of water. He was dehydrated and needed the liquid.

Ephram had given him an idea, though he was not enthused about it. Leaning over the sink, Shane forced two fingers to the back of his mouth as far as he could reach. His throat convulsed, and his stomach followed suit. A quick gush of water and bile erupted over his hand. In the sink, in a foamy puddle, the two partially dissolved pills were stuck together.

Shane rinsed them down the drain and cleaned his hand and mouth. He was keeping his head clear. At least he thought he was. He just needed to get back to one hundred percent without Dr. Loomis realizing it.

"Sneaky," the ghost said after he left the bathroom. He clutched the door frame again, holding it like a shield between himself and Shane.

The redhead had returned as well, still hiding in the corner, and watching Shane intently. They were not the best roommates, but they were something.

Despite himself, Shane felt drowsiness overcoming him once more. He wanted to fight it, to stay awake and try to plan a way out, but his body betrayed him. He hadn't even realized that he had laid back down. In seconds, his eyes were closed again.

When he opened his eyes, the room was still lit through the tiny window, but the angle had changed considerably. He must have been asleep for at least five hours. A tray of food sat on the floor next to his door, and the bathroom ghost scuttled back to the doorway the moment he realized Shane was conscious.

"You got a name?" Shane asked, sitting up.

His head swam from the movement. He reminded himself to take things a little more slowly going forward until he was back to himself. His mind was much clearer, however, and though he still felt deeply relaxed and somewhat drowsy, it was nowhere near as bad as it had been.

"Who's asking?" the bathroom ghost asked suspiciously.

Shane laughed as he glanced at the food. There was white bread, possibly some sort of sandwich, a fruit cup, and a cup of juice. Not high cuisine, but he was surprised they were feeding him at all.

"I can just call you 'Toilet' if you want," he told the ghost.

He stood, weakness causing his legs to wobble, and took a moment to get steady. For the first time, he realized he was not wearing the clothes in which he'd been arrested. Someone had changed him into gray sweatpants and a light blue T-shirt. Even his boots had been swapped out. He now wore red tube socks with grippy material on the soles.

"Not Toilet," the bathroom ghost growled. "Jester. Name is Jester!"

"Is it?"

Shane did not believe anyone had ever called that man or his ghost Jester, but it was all he had to go on. Jester nodded emphatically, and Shane shrugged and retrieved his food.

"They put anything in this?" he asked.

"Turkey roll and margarine," Jester replied as though revealing a dark secret.

Shane opened the sandwich, and it was as the ghost described. Drab, beige meat, and a smear of yellowish grease on plain, white bread that was stiff and probably a day or two old. He had eaten worse.

The sandwich had no flavor beyond mild saltiness, and the orange juice was watered down. Even the fruit cup lacked anything beyond a hint of peachy flavor in the tepid water. But it was food, and it seemed untainted. Shane needed the energy.

An orderly came to take the tray some hours later and told Shane that next time, he should push it out of the slot into the hallway. He mumbled something and pretended to be sleepy, and the man left without another word.

"Deceptive," Jester said.

Shane was on the bed, lying on his back and staring at the ceiling. There was nothing to do in the room, nor could he do anything without giving away the fact that he had not taken his medication.

"Who came by last night?" he asked as the day gave way to evening. "That clicking in the hall that you and the redhead were so afraid of."

"Nothing," Jester told him. "Don't want to meet him. The devil. The devil himself."

"Is that his name?"

"Doesn't have a name. Has every name! The devil is in the details," Jester whispered. Shane sighed. Things would be easier if the redheaded ghost's jaw weren't wired shut.

Several minutes passed, and when Shane didn't speak again, Jester scuttled out of the bathroom for the first time since they had met while Shane was conscious and aware of him.

"Need to be careful," the ghost said softly. "He comes every night."

His eagerness to speak had overcome his eagerness to be difficult and offer Shane useless answers.

"Why?" Shane asked, still staring at the ceiling.

Jester scuttled closer until he was at the foot of the bed. He hid most of his body behind it, resting his hands on either side of the corner near Shane's foot and peeking over the edge.

"To hurt," the ghost answered. "He likes to hurt."

For the first time, Jester spoke in a sincere voice. While he was being coy or effusive before, or just plain confusing, his words now rang true. The ghost in the hall was something dangerous.

A tray with dinner came several hours later. Shane could smell it before he saw it, the unpleasant odor of microwaved fish. A flabby, white filet sat on a plate next to lima beans and some kind of brown mash.

Shane ate the food and didn't think about the taste. He pushed the tray back out the slot halfway, making it look like he was too tired or too fuzzy to have effectively managed the job.

The redheaded ghost came and went throughout the evening. Unable to speak, she would simply watch. When he spoke to her, she offered little in the way of feedback. Jester said nothing about her. Their little triumvirate was not very impressive.

With the drugs still in his system, Shane closed his eyes at some point, and when he opened them, it was morning again. Dr. Loomis stood over his bed once more with Ephram behind him.

"How are you feeling today, Shane? You've been eating; that's good."

"Good," Shane said, blinking and trying to focus.

"How about the medication? Any side effects you want to tell me about?"

"Good," he said again, trying to sit up.

Dr. Loomis smiled and handed him another small cup of pills. Shane took them, downed them quickly, and then swallowed the water. Ephram grabbed his face again and forced his mouth open. The pills were gone.

"Very good, Shane. I'm happy to see that. I had been led to believe you would be much more difficult to deal with, but look at you, already right in step with everything," Dr. Loomis said.

Despite the doctor's praise, Ephram punched Shane in the stomach and then slapped his head to force him back down on the bed. Shane made sounds of protestation but offered little fight. They needed to think the pills were working.

Dr. Loomis jotted some notes on his chart and looked at his phone.

"Just a few more days, Shane, then you won't have to worry about Ephram anymore. I think it's time to start the rest of your treatment."

Shane grunted and rolled over in the bed. The doctor and Ephram left.

"Bad," Jester said.

The ghost was back in the bathroom. Shane waited a minute before getting to his feet again and heading there himself. The ghost hid beside the toilet when Shane entered rather than vanishing. As he had done the day before, Shane forced fingers down his throat and vomited the pills.

"What's bad?" Shane asked after wiping his mouth.

"Treatment," Jester explained. "Don't want treatment."

"So I've gathered."

Shane headed back to the bed and sat while Jester came back to the door.

"What is this place, Jester? This isn't a legit hospital. It can't be."

The ghost giggled, the sound off-putting and childish coming from his droopy, wrinkled face.

"Bad things can happen anywhere if everyone looks the other way," he explained. He wasn't wrong, nor was he very helpful.

"Why were you here?"

"To die," Jester explained. "To hurt and to die."

CHAPTER 9
TREATMENT

No one came to see Shane for the rest of the day. He skipped lunch to make it seem like he was still sleeping but ate dinner. Jester sat freely at the foot of the bed for the bulk of the day, talking whether Shane wanted him to or not.

When Jester moved, Shane could see he had suffered some serious injury in life. His body was broken and awkward, hunched, and misshapen. He walked more like an ape than a man, bent and using his arms to help him along.

The ghost did not have anything very interesting or important to share, but it was clear it had been some time since he'd spoken to anyone. He told Shane about all the menu items the hospital provided for various meals. He told Shane about how the clothes they provided used to look different. Sometimes, he went off on a dark tangent and told Shane about people he had seen die.

"What's Dr. Loomis doing here? He working for Hawkins or Silvershore?"

"Don't know shores of silver," Jester said, shaking his head. "Don't know a hawk man."

Shane had established that Dr. Loomis had a history of appearing to treat patients and then ultimately killing them off. He could only go by the disjointed information Jester provided. Nothing made sense, but the ghost was adamant that Shane was not meant to leave the hospital alive. Shane didn't need a ghost to tell him that, but he wanted to know why Hawkins was drawing it out. If they wanted him dead, why didn't they kill him on the first day?

The pretense of caring about his mental health and giving him medication to treat a condition he didn't have didn't make sense. It was possible they just wanted to keep him out of the way and sedated, but to what end? That was something either Dr. Loomis or Hawkins would have to answer, but Shane didn't suspect either would volunteer information anytime soon.

The redheaded ghost came back from time to time, but she only stared at Shane silently from the corner. He tried to get her to do anything to indicate she understood him but got nothing.

If she had been a patient in the hospital like Jester, then her end probably had not come easily. Her jaw being wired shut must have been torture. Shane wondered if she had been a patient of Dr. Loomis, and if Ephram had been responsible for her jaw. He had too much time to wonder about such things, alone in his room as he was.

When the sun set, the room went dark. Very slowly, Jester had been making his way from the end of the bed to the far side of the room, opposite the door. He wasn't ready to escape to the bathroom just yet, but it was clear to Shane that he wanted some distance between himself and the hallway.

Hours passed, and Shane fought to stay awake. Though he hadn't taken the pills, whatever shot he had been given that first day still hadn't fully worn off.

He had never felt this tired, certainly not so easily when he knew he needed to stay awake. He didn't like what it had done to him but couldn't think of a way to fight the effect. All he could do was avoid the pills and wait it out.

Long after the hospital had gone quiet and the night had settled in, the clicking sound from the hallway started again.

Click.

It was far from his room, as it had been the last time Shane heard it.

Seconds passed and then another click sounded. Then another. And another.

A quick flash of movement on Shane's right was the only indication he had that Jester had left, vanishing as though he always did whenever the clicking sound started.

The clicking grew closer.

Click… click… click.

The sound reached a door very close to Shane's. He gathered his thoughts and focus, to prepare himself in case something happened. His mind began to wander as he pondered over what made the sound, then where Jester had gone, and what happened to the orderlies from when he was admitted.

It was a long moment before Shane shook his head and realized he had lost his train of thought. How much time had passed since he heard the last click? He couldn't remember. Had it just been a moment? A whole minute? Ten?

Shane was staring up at the ceiling, and the sound had stopped. He rolled over in bed to look at the door, to focus on the tiny window in case something passed; a shadow, like it had the day before. There was no window to view this time. The shadow was there, but it was inside the room and blocking the door.

It was the shape of a man, just standing in the darkness in front of his door. Black on black, it was hard to determine if it was anyone he had seen before. For now, it was merely a shape.

The shadowy form moved, and Shane made out an arm. The spirit dragged a hand across the inside of his door until its fingernails reached the hinges with a loud click.

Without warning, the shape moved. It was on top of Shane in the blink of an eye, and he made out more of the figure. The ghost had been that of a man about Shane's height, with a mane of ragged, dirty blond hair hanging over his face.

Shane could see multiple scars in the pale flesh, not the result of accidents, but intentional cuts all over the spirit's face. It looked as though the blade of a knife or a razor had been used to create a patchwork of scars across every exposed skin.

Two of the largest scars went from the corners of the ghost's mouth and up his cheeks. Two more ran from his forehead down over his eyes, and then down his cheeks on either side of his nose.

The ghost held Shane down by his arms and, even in the tangle of hair, Shane could see that his eyes had been sliced open.

Shane struggled in the ghost's grip, and he felt the cold hands squeeze his wrists tightly. The ghost's arm jerked, and he raised Shane's hand just enough to thrust it back, forcing Shane to punch himself in the face.

The spirit was humming, making strange noises as it repeated the gesture with Shane's other hand.

Shane's muscles were incredibly weak. He pulled away, but the exhaustion in his body made it feel like he had spent the entire day working out and was now too spent to put in any effort. Just trying to pull away from the ghost felt like he was trying to lift a car.

The ghost didn't speak, he just hummed and held fast, preventing Shane from getting the upper hand. At one point, he leaned in and bit Shane's forearm. Teeth like ice punctured the flesh as Shane started to scream, but the ghost forced Shane's hand over his mouth to muffle it.

When the spirit pulled away, Shane saw blood running down his arm. Every crooked tooth had plunged into the flesh, but he had not taken a chunk. Instead, he had left a perfect imprint of his maw, marking Shane.

The ghost continued to hum softly and lifted Shane's left hand. He took one of Shane's fingers between his lips and bit down hard on the nail, pulling it until it tore away from the nail bed.

Shane's body jerked but refused to respond the way it should have. He was powerless against a ghost that sought to torment him. He could feel his muscles straining, trying to work, but every flex was like lifting a thousand-pound weight.

The fingernail ripped off, and the sharp pain that shot down his arm was like burning electricity. He cried out between clenched teeth, and the ghost dropped his hand, pressing down over his face.

He saw the mouth open, broken and stained teeth coming for his face, and he froze as the ghost's gaping jaws settled over his left eye. He didn't dare move as the ghost stopped, not following through on its threat.

The world had gone black over Shane's eye. He felt cold teeth like icicles, and the air coming from the ghost's mouth threatened to freeze his eyeball. All he had to do was clamp down, and he'd bite into Shane's cheek and eyebrow. If he had enough force, he'd be able to bite Shane's eye right from his face.

The humming began again, and Shane held as still as a statue. He didn't understand what the ghost was doing or why, but it was too powerful for him to fight in his condition. He needed more time.

With a silent anger twisting in his gut, Shane relaxed completely. He let his arms go limp and lay there, not struggling or defending himself.

The spirit stayed where he was, pressed against Shane's body, mouth locked over his eye socket. Shane felt something probe his face, cold and sloppy. The ghost's tongue pushed into his eye socket, plunging into the corner, and then sliding across the eye's surface like a slug. Shane clenched his jaw but didn't resist.

He sensed the ghost was waiting to punish him for fighting back. It was like Dr. Loomis himself, expecting Shane to act a certain way so he could be corrected in whatever brutal manner he found appropriate. Shane would not play this round.

The ghost stopped humming and slowly pulled away. The tangle of hair hung between them, tickling Shane's face. In the darkness, Shane could barely make out the spirit's expression, but it seemed emotionless. It was neither pleased nor disappointed. It was blank and unreadable.

The sliced eyes stared into Shane's, and the ghost produced a curious sound the way a dog might when confronted with something unexpected. Shane made no sound and did not move.

The ghost began humming again as it slipped away, slowly and awkwardly walking backward toward the door. Shane didn't turn his head to watch him go.

Click.

The sound had returned to the hallway.

Click… click… click.

The ghost continued on his rounds, getting farther and farther from Shane's room.

"He likes to hurt," Jester said, reappearing at the foot of Shane's bed.

"Yeah," Shane said quietly. The pain in his finger had died down, and the bite on his arm had settled into a tolerable burning sensation.

Jester ambled closer to the side of the bed, and Shane felt something light fall on his leg. Jester had brought him a cloth from the bathroom.

"Thanks," he said, wrapping it around his finger to staunch the bleeding.

"Good to hide the blood," Jester said softly. "Hide the blood, hide the hurt."

"Good thinking," Shane said. Exhaustion overwhelmed him; failing to overcome the ghost had drained him.

Sleep came soon despite the pain.

CHAPTER 10

IT COMES AT NIGHT

"Oh my goodness, Shane. What did you do to yourself?"

Dr. Loomis was standing over Shane in his room. He opened his eyes and looked up at the man, feeling the ache in his face, arms, and hand. He felt more focused and aware than he had the previous day, but he was not sure if his strength was coming back in any practical way.

"Bad night," he said.

"You cannot hurt yourself like this," Dr. Loomis continued. "Why did you do this?"

Shane grunted softly. Dr. Loomis was baiting him, asking him to say that a ghost had done it. He didn't understand the doctor's game, but he did not want to play it.

"I don't know," he answered. Dr. Loomis tsked and shook his head, scribbling some notes.

"This cannot become a habit, Shane. If you keep hurting yourself, something will have to be done to stop it. Restraints or maybe medical intervention. You don't want that, do you?"

"No. I don't," Shane agreed.

Dr. Loomis nodded and jotted more notes, then handed over the pills. Shane got up slowly and took the cup, swallowing two pills and the water. Before Ephram could reach him, he opened his mouth wide to show there was nothing in it. It made him feel like a child, but there was some degree of satisfaction in seeing the annoyed look on the big man's face. It was the first sign of emotion he'd shown.

"Very good, Shane. Ephram, give Shane a reward for being so

cooperative this morning."

Ephram's look of displeasure became the subtlest of smiles. His fist struck Shane square in the face and knocked him back onto the pillow.

"Please take care of yourself, Shane. We will have to advance to more extreme treatment if I can't trust that you're caring for your well-being."

The two men left the room and locked the door behind them. Shane sighed and raised a hand to his face, pulling away his fingers to look at the blood running from his nose.

The way Dr. Loomis spoke was very unsettling. Not the words he used, but the fact that he sounded so sincerely concerned when he spoke them. That he would talk to Shane as though worried about him even as Ephram punched him in the face was hard to reconcile. The man gave no indication that he enjoyed the torture he put Shane through, or even that he wanted it to happen.

"Will be worse tonight," Jester said, appearing in the bathroom doorway.

Shane nodded and passed the ghost on the way to the sink. Jester didn't skulk away this time, he only leaned back so Shane didn't come close enough to touch him.

Once again, Shane vomited into the sink. He washed up after, taking care to clean the bite, his missing nail, and his nose.

Dr. Loomis, for all his faux concern, had not made any attempt to dress the wounds or even leave something Shane could use to cover them. The bite on his arm was unlikely to get infected, at least. A small upside to being bitten by something non-corporeal. Ghosts did not carry bacteria.

Shane ate breakfast when it came, then lunch. He could have still pretended that he was unfocused and disorganized, but he realized he needed more strength and clarity. The scarred spirit was more of a problem than Dr. Loomis.

He walked around the small room, getting his heart rate up and his blood pumping. It was not intense exercise, and he didn't want to strain himself, he just wanted to work his muscles and make them feel alive again.

Jester watched him work and talked to him about the hospital and other patients.

"They go sometimes," the ghost said. "Go side. Dead side. Put you on dead side."

Shane nodded. He had developed a sense of understanding when it came to the vague way Jester spoke. If he had to guess, he thought that the hospital ran legitimately for some patients, but Hawkins and maybe other interested parties used the rest of the facilities, and the staff, to do dirty work for them.

Hawkins had done fairly well using military resources, so taking advantage of a psychiatric hospital would probably have been very easy. Money did not seem to be an issue for Reaper Company, so all Hawkins needed was one unscrupulous doctor willing to do things for a payday. He had found that in Dr. Loomis.

Still, there were holes in the story. Why Dr. Loomis kept up the act was something Shane didn't understand. No one else was coming to check on him, so there was no reason to pretend. Someone wanted Shane alive but in pain. Maybe it was Hawkins. Maybe the man just wanted to torture him, and this is what he came up with.

It didn't make any difference whose idea it was, or why they were doing it. Shane's goals remained the same. Escape, put an end to Dr. Loomis and Hawkins, put the Reapers in the ground forever.

Shane continued his walk. He paused often to drink water from the bathroom sink, to flush his system further. The hours he had before nightfall were ticking away. The ghost with the scarred face was coming back; he would bet money on it.

"Tell me more about Scarface," Shane said, cutting off Jester in the midst of a story about electroconvulsive therapy.

"Scarface? What Scarface?"

"The ghost who came for me last night. How long has he been here?

Who else has he hurt?"

"Forever," Jester said with an indignant snort as though it were obvious. "Been here always. Hurts everyone. Everyone gets it eventually. Everyone has to hurt."

"Does he have a real name? Can he talk?"

"Scarface," Jester said. "Name's Scarface."

Shane gave up on trying to get answers. He let Jester ramble on some more while he continued to walk and drink. The process was slow, but he felt stronger. His muscles no longer had a run-down, rubbery feeling. His mind felt sharper. Not one hundred percent, but closer. Close enough to maybe fight back next time.

He ate dinner when it came and then returned to his bed to relax and come up with a plan.

"Might kill you tonight," Jester said. He had advanced to the side of the bed now, down by Shane's knees. It was closer than Shane wanted him to be, but as long as he didn't get much closer, it was fine.

"Hoping to avoid it," Shane replied.

"No one has."

"Not yet."

"Not yet," Jester repeated. "Not yet. Not yet."

The sun set, and Shane felt his tension rise. He didn't know if he was well enough to take on Scarface. The only way to find out would be when it happened. He didn't like leaving things like that up to chance, but he would roll the dice.

Jester talked non-stop. He was in the middle of a story about boxes in the basement that held secrets when the clicking sound interrupted him.

The ghost was gone instantly. He stopped speaking mid-sentence and when Shane glanced down in the darkness of the room, Jester had vanished.

Click.

"Try not to die," Jester whispered. He was under the bed. Shane said nothing in reply.

Click.

He waited as patiently as he could, forcing a calm onto himself. The clicking continued closer and closer until finally, it reached Shane's door. He was watching this time. A shadow seeped through the metal of the door and coalesced into the shape of a man. Scarface had returned. Shane sat up to greet him.

"You sure you want to do this again?" he asked.

Scarface began humming and then, just as the night before, rushed at Shane with no warning. Shane took a knee immediately, on the floor in front of his bed.

It was hard to estimate the blow in the darkness, especially since Scarface concealed himself in shadow, but Shane did his best. His fist lashed out and collided with the side of the ghost's knee as he put his weight down just a step from Shane.

The ghost gasped, breaking his humming routine, and collapsed. His momentum and the angle of his leg caused it to snap at the knee. Shane was on him in an instant, lifting the ghost's still-functional leg and bringing it down the wrong way over his knee.

Scarface gasped, just an exhalation rather than a scream, and his other leg snapped. Shane held it tightly, his left arm curled around the broken segment, then dropped and rolled. The leg tore free at the knee and dissolved in Shane's grasp as he got back to his feet and faced the ghost.

With one leg missing below the knee and the other leg broken, Scarface could not stand. The ghost awkwardly balanced himself on one broken limb and one stump, holding the side of Shane's bed to stay steady.

His dirty-looking hair still covered most of his face, but Shane could see him clearly enough to know that the ghost was enraged. The split eyes had locked on Shane, and the ghost's expression was pure, cold fury.

"You look like you want to say something," Shane said.

He could see that the scars that covered the ghost's face extended down his throat, where they were thicker and deeper. He guessed that the ghost had severed vocal cords and lost the ability to speak. Though it was petty, Shane found it amusing to mock him for it, anyway.

Scarface was tense, and Shane could see he was plotting what to do next. Barely three feet separated them, but Shane had the upper hand now. Scarface was not used to someone fighting back. And now, he was permanently crippled, something he had not expected.

"Trying to think of your next move?" Shane grinned at the ghost. "I'll take your arms next. And since you like those teeth so much, I'll take them, too. I will turn you into a goddamn canoe, so please, by all means, try it again."

It was hard to read Scarface's eyes, split down the middle as they were, but Shane felt like there was some doubt there now. He didn't know how long the ghost had terrorized the hospital, but it had been long enough to make other spirits like the redhead and Jester afraid. Now that the tables were turned, the ghost didn't know what to do.

Scarface opened his mouth and hissed. His tongue was split down the middle, and each side operated independently. The ghost then darted left, crawling back toward the door and out of the room. He was gone in a blink, and there were no more clicks to indicate his passage as he left.

Shane waited for several minutes before moving. When he felt confident that the ghost was not coming back, he returned to the bed, sitting on the side facing the door.

"How?" Jester asked.

He was at the foot of the bed now, looking at Shane as though seeing something miraculous.

"Old trick," Shane replied.

"No," Jester said, shaking his head. "Changes everything. This is everything! Hurt him. Hurt Scarface."

"Would have done more if he hadn't skittered away," Shane said. It would have made his stay in the hospital a little easier if he'd just crushed him. He hadn't expected the ghost to run off so soon.

"Don't know this," Jester said, more to himself than to Shane. "Never seen this."

"Yeah. I'm full of surprises."

Shane lay back down in bed and listened for signs of the ghost's return. Eventually, sleep overtook him. When he awoke the next morning, it was to Ephram's fists pummeling his face.

CHAPTER 11

ESCALATION

Shane rolled over and spit out blood on sheets as the big orderly took a step back. He had punched Shane in the face multiple times; he wasn't entirely sure how many since he had woken up in the middle of it.

Dr. Loomis stood where he always stood with his clipboard in hand, only this time he did not bother to read it. Instead, he stared at Shane with a look of disappointment on his face.

"I thought we were making progress," Dr. Loomis said wistfully.

Shane spit on the floor at the doctor's feet and then wiped his mouth as he sat up.

"Did something happen that makes you think otherwise?" Shane asked.

He knew that Dr. Loomis was not about to admit that he sent Scarface down the hall every night. That wouldn't fit his strange, fictional narrative as a concerned doctor dealing with a mental patient.

"With your habit of hurting yourself, and your agitated mental state, I can't help but feel like something more needs to be done. In the interest of keeping you safe," Dr. Loomis said.

"I can't wait," Shane replied.

Dr. Loomis could only smile. He nodded, and Ephram pushed Shane back onto the bed and rolled him onto his stomach. A second orderly must have joined them from the hall, but Shane could not see who it was.

Shane was forced to roll first to the left and then to the right as a piece of rough, thick fabric was pulled tight against him. He felt his hands being guided into sleeves and got a look at the garment that they were dressing him in. He was being placed into a straitjacket.

Belts and straps were fastened tightly around Shane as his hands were pulled in opposite directions, forcing him to essentially hug himself. The straps were secured along his arms and across his midsection, and an extra one was pulled up between his legs and secured at the back to ensure he couldn't wriggle free.

When the orderlies were finished, Ephram rolled him over again and then slapped him across the face. Dr. Loomis handed the cup of pills to the orderly, and the big man pulled Shane up by the straitjacket and dumped the pills into his mouth.

He wasn't given any water this time; instead, Ephram just pinched his nose closed and held his mouth shut tightly, tilting Shane's head back until he swallowed the pills. When he was finished, the orderly pushed him down onto the bed and walked away.

"I hope you're more responsive tomorrow, Shane. Things can escalate very quickly if you force my hand."

Dr. Loomis and Ephram left together and locked the door. Shane sat up and struggled against the straitjacket. When he pulled one arm, it tightened the other side. If he moved forward, it pulled him from the back. He had seen magicians force their way out of straitjackets, but he didn't know the trick, and Ephram had pulled it very tight at every belt and buckle.

Aggravated, he made his way to the bathroom to choke out the pills he had been forced to take. Without being able to use his fingers, he struggled and forced himself to dry heave, but nothing happened.

"Not good," Jester said, crouched low to the ground near Shane's leg. "Not good."

"I need your help," Shane told the ghost. "I need you to get this thing off of me."

The ghost grimaced and held himself close as though he were wearing a straitjacket as well. Shane turned his back and then looked over his shoulder.

"Just pull some of these buckles loose," he said.

Hesitantly, Jester waddled forward and held out his hand. It looked like he was about to do as Shane asked when he flinched and pulled away.

"Can't," the ghost said, shaking his wrinkled head. "Can't touch."

"You can," Shane insisted.

"Iron!" the ghost shouted, then covered his mouth. "Iron buckles."

Shane cursed and looked in the mirror. The only reason for there to be iron buckles on a straitjacket was if someone had made it specifically to be untouchable by ghosts.

"Then I need you to do something else," Shane requested.

Jester cocked his head to one side.

"Can't touch iron," he explained.

"I need you to help me puke."

Jester grimaced again, and Shane repositioned himself over the sink.

"You need to be fast, before I digest them."

"Doesn't sound right," Jester said with a shake of his head.

"Jester, I am going to die tonight if I'm drugged and in this jacket. Even without legs, Scarface can kill me like this. Help me."

"Help," Jester repeated. "I gotta help. You gotta puke."

Jester stood for the first time, his body rickety and shaky. His spine curved badly to one side, and he thrust a hand at Shane's face. Shane wanted it less than the ghost, but it was the only thing he could think of on short notice.

Fingers like frozen sausages pushed to the back of his throat. They alternated between feeling smooth and gritty, but the cold and thickness of them was something completely foreign.

Shane choked and then brought up the pills while Jester groaned and pulled away, shaking his hand as though he had been tainted.

"Turn this on, please," Shane asked, spitting into the sink. The ghost obliged by turning on the faucet, and Shane leaned down to rinse out his mouth.

"Never want to do that again," he said to himself afterward.

"No. Not good," Jester agreed.

Shane shuffled back to his bed, struggling against his bonds with no progress. Things were escalating out of his hands. He had hoped that avoiding the medication would give him some kind of advantage, but that had been stripped away.

No meals were brought to Shane that day. He stayed with Jester and thought of something he could do to get word out of the hospital, or escape the room the next time Dr. Loomis and Ephram came in. None of his ideas were practical. He was left with nothing.

Time ticked by, and no one came to check on him; not that he expected it. Bound as he was, he couldn't even take care of simple bodily functions. The straitjacket was meant as a punishment and an indignity. Shane took it in stride as well as he could.

He realized that Dr. Loomis was trying to break him on some level. If the result wasn't Shane being dead, it would be him locked away somewhere forever, maybe grievously wounded, or crippled. The rules of the game were not in his favor.

Shane scraped the straitjacket against the corner of the bed, the edge of his table, and the wardrobe. Nothing was sharp enough to wear it down. He wasted hours struggling and was no closer to being free than when he started that morning.

The day dragged on and on. Now that his head was clear, he was able to appreciate the passage of time, and it seemed to take an eternity. Night arrived slowly and ominously.

"It's dark," Jester said, as though Shane couldn't tell. "Dark and dangerous. Darkly dangerous."

The ghost fretted and rocked slightly at the foot of the bed.

"He might not come back," Shane said.

Scarface was only one of his concerns, of course. But it would be nice to get through the night without another visit from the angry ghost.

The night progressed slowly, but Shane had no way to tell the time. At least when the sun was up, he could watch the movement of the light through the window. Now, all he could do was guess.

He was certain it had reached the time when Scarface normally appeared, but nothing happened. Shane waited and waited. He saw nothing and heard nothing.

Shane strained to hear any sounds. A faint humming came through the floors, something electrical and distant. Every so often, he heard what sounded like a drip echoing somewhere, up through the pipes in his bathroom. There were no sounds of life, nor had there been since he arrived. There was no indication that the rooms near him were occupied by living people.

It seemed like Shane was alone in the ward, or each room had been well soundproofed. Neither would have surprised him; both seemed like the sort of thing Dr. Loomis would do.

The first vestiges of dawn begin to illuminate the sky outside of his window. Black faded to a navy bluish gray. Shane had made it through the night.

Something tugged at the bed sheets beneath Shane's leg. He looked down, expecting to see Jester huddled at the foot of the bed. Instead, freezing claws sank into his thigh as he saw Scarface pull himself up from the floor.

Shane leaned forward as the ghost clawed his way up, latching onto whatever he could to get closer. All Shane could do in defense was rock his body from side to side and try to shake off the ghost, but Scarface held fast.

The humming began as Scarface pulled himself even with Shane until they were looking at each other in the eye. His useless legs dangled behind him, but the intensity in his bisected eyes was unmistakable. Even though the ghost couldn't speak, the rage on his face spoke volumes.

Scarface opened his mouth, showing off his teeth and split tongue. He leaned closer to Shane, moving with measured steadiness, inching closer to prolong Shane's torment even as his mouth spread wider.

The long, lanky hair spilled onto Shane's face, and he felt breath puffing in blasts like gusts of winter air across his nose and eyes. Scarface's mouth was less than an inch away from clamping down on Shane, biting into his cheek, his eyebrow, or even plucking the eye from his skull as the ghost threatened to do at their first meeting.

To reach Shane's eye, the ghost had to extend himself further. He had to raise his head above Shane's. His pale, scarred throat was now even with Shane's mouth.

While Scarface liked to play games and drive the torment, Shane only wanted to survive. He did not hesitate.

Shane sank his teeth into the ghost's neck. It felt spongy and chewy at the same time, a strange, cold thickness with an impossible-to-describe texture. There was no taste.

He clamped his jaws as tightly as he could, forcing his teeth together around the spectral tissue. Scarface pulled back instinctively and cost himself a mouthful of flesh in the process.

With the ghost unbalanced, Shane bucked his hips and then rolled, knocking the ghost aside and getting on top of it as they fell to the floor. He used his feet to push forward and angled his elbows inside the straitjacket as best he could to keep himself even.

Scarface produced a hissing sound as Shane dove for the ghost's neck, angling for the original bite that had left a chunk of his insides exposed. Shane caught a glimpse of the ghost's esophagus and muscle tissue. It was like an "X" on a map.

He gnashed his teeth and bit deeper, the strange non-living tissue giving way easily under the assault. Scarface clawed at his back, but Shane bit hard on something more solid than what he had felt. He had found the ghost's spine.

Wrenching his head back, Shane held his teeth together as tightly as he could. Something snapped inside Scarface's neck, and the hissing sound ended abruptly. The ghost's head snapped backward, and Shane pulled a segment of spinal column free.

The chunk of bone vanished in Shane's mouth, and the ghost went limp beneath him. He could see Scarface's eyes still moving and his lips trying to form a sound, but his body had been crippled.

Without hands, Shane could not finish the job easily. He could try to use his shoulder. He could force his body weight onto the ghost's skull and crush it, putting the monster out of its misery.

Another thought occurred to Shane. He could just leave Scarface like that. Crippled for eternity, unable to move or speak ever again. It was the cruelest torture he could imagine. However, he would also be on the floor of the room that Shane was in for an indeterminate amount of time. He wasn't sure he wanted that sort of roommate.

"Look here," Jester said, creeping around the end of the bed. "Just look here."

Shane struggled to sit up, working his body far too intensely to get onto his knees and flop back against the bed. His breath came in exhausted gasps as he rested his head on the mattress side, his legs extended next to Scarface on the floor.

"Couldn't quite finish the job," Shane explained. "Give me a minute."

"Oh, yes. Not finished," Jester whispered. He moved closer still, creeping alongside Scarface on his haunches as he held a hand over the other ghost, almost but not quite touching him.

Shane watched as the old, wrinkled ghost's hand hovered over Scarface's legs and then moved all the way up the torso. He stopped when he reached the ghost's shredded and half-missing neck.

"Look. At. This," Jester whispered.

Jester lifted his head and looked at Shane. There were tears in his eyes, and his rumpled, old face expressed a deep anguish. Behind him, the redheaded ghost had crept from the shadows, barely visible in the first light of day. There were other spirits, too, ones Shane had never seen. They huddled in the bathroom door, and along the wall, watching.

"Want to hurt him," Jester said. "He made me. Owe him such hurt."

His voice was pleading, and he stared at Shane like a beggar asking for change.

"Do what you need to do," Shane said.

Jester smiled, and tears ran from his eyes. He lowered his head and lifted one of Scarface's lifeless arms.

"Hurt," the ghost said. He snapped the smallest finger off Scarface's hand.

"Hurt," he said again, taking the next finger in line.

The redhead came forward then and knelt. Jester looked at her but said nothing. She went for Scarface's mouth, reached in, and crushed his jaw in her fist, pulling out a handful of teeth and casting them aside.

The other spirits converged, and a massacre began. They tore Scarface apart, pulling out his insides and removing pieces bit by bit until someone finally tipped the scales.

What remained of Scarface exploded and knocked all the spirits back. Shane could only wince and turn his head, unable to avoid the force of the blow, and when he looked back, nothing remained of Scarface.

The redhead had been knocked back to the door, and Jester scuttled forward again from the foot of the bed. The others drifted back into the shadows as mysteriously as they had arrived.

"Good," Jester said. "Need to leave now. Or there will be punishment."

CHAPTER 12

THE PROCEDURE

Dr. Loomis walked down the long, empty stretch of hallway toward his office. His right shoe pinched his feet at the toes, and it was annoying. He kept forgetting to buy a new pair. He would have to tell his secretary to put it in his schedule.

His footsteps echoed in the empty space, the linoleum making them sound almost like a horse clip-clopping down the hall. He reached the door to his office and pulled out the key to unlock it, discovering that it was already open.

Dr. Loomis made a habit of locking the door before he left. To find it open was not expected. If someone had broken in, he would have security in the entire building fired.

He pushed the door open cautiously and looked into his office. The man sitting in the chair at his desk smiled.

"Well, hey, Doc. How are you?" Brett Hawkins asked, absently playing with a familiar wooden box.

Dr. Loomis set down his clipboard and nodded, taking one of the uncomfortable chairs on the opposite side of his desk.

"Mr. Hawkins. I'm well, and you?"

"Peachy keen, Doc. Peachy keen. So, listen, I got your fifteen goddamn messages. You want to tell me what was so urgent that I had to rush over here and interrupt this beautiful Wednesday morning?"

Dr. Loomis had not sent Hawkins fifteen messages, but he had sent several that had gone unanswered. He had taken Shane Ryan as a patient based on Hawkins' urging, but the man had offered no additional feedback on what was to happen.

Ryan was extremely disruptive. The longer they kept a patient in the hospital who wasn't allowed to interact with anyone else, the more red flags would go up. Someone would eventually come looking for him, and someone would have to provide answers.

"There was a problem with Dudley," Dr. Loomis said.

Hawkins, relaxed in Dr. Loomis' ergonomic, high-backed chair, remained stone-faced.

"Two nights ago, Ryan destroyed his legs."

Hawkins laughed loudly and shook his head while tossing the wooden box back and forth between his hands.

"That's the sort of thing Ryan does," he replied. "Sounds like you're not giving him enough medication."

"I've been giving him a high dose. He should be more sedate than he is, but I'm hesitant to force more on him in case of adverse side effects."

"Adverse side effects," Hawkins repeated mockingly. "God forbid."

"You said you wanted to keep him alive," Dr. Loomis reminded the other man.

Hawkins sighed and rolled his eyes.

"I did. Is this all you've got for me? I came down here because your little ghoulie got his legs broken? How is this anything I need to care about? Tie him to the bed if you're so worried. You're the professional here; you figure it out."

"I put Ryan in a straitjacket," Dr. Loomis continued. "And last night, he destroyed Dudley."

Hawkins fixed Dr. Loomis with a level stare and leaned in close, his elbows on the desk.

"He destroyed him?"

"From what I can tell. Dudley is gone, and some of the night crew made note of a vibration, like an explosion or a crash just before shift change."

"He's still in the straitjacket?" Hawkins asked.

"He is."

Hawkins laughed again. He threw his head back and made it a dramatic, unnecessary belly laugh while Dr. Loomis waited for him to quiet down and continue.

"That boy, I'll tell you what," Hawkins said, still chuckling. "I would have given my right leg to get him on board back when we started this thing."

"You tried?" Dr. Loomis asked.

"No," Hawkins said sharply. "Ryan was never going to be a Reaper. I wonder sometimes if that man was born with a stick up his ass. He's not the kind to bend to fit a new mold; to do things a new way. You can see in his eyes that he doesn't like following orders. He'll do it—he did it as a Marine—but you can see the gears turning in there. He thinks for himself too much."

Dr. Loomis did not reply. He was not involved enough in Hawkins' endeavors to waste time worrying about a rogue soldier looking for him one day.

"Who do you have there?" he asked of the box in Hawkins' hands.

"I need something new. Personal security."

"Is Cathcart not acceptable?"

"No, no, he's fine," Hawkins said. "But he's gross, Doc. He stinks, and he brings bugs and toilet water wherever he goes. I need a bodyguard, not a mobile swamp."

"Did you bring him back?"

Hawkins chuckled, looking at Dr. Loomis like he was a fool.

"This isn't a bottle return, Dr. Loomis. You make the soldiers, I take them. I don't bring them back. Your predecessor knows that, and you should, too. Cathcart and his swamp of horrors will have his place, but I needed something more personal. Close range. So, I snagged this one."

Dr. Loomis frowned. Most of the boxes from the basement looked identical. Only the nametags differentiated them, save for some size differences based on what was inside. But Hawkins was playing coy, and that could only mean one thing.

"He's going to be hard to control," Dr. Loomis said.

"Let me worry about that."

"What do you want done with Ryan?" Dr. Loomis asked, changing the subject.

"For a doctor, you don't have a lot of patience," Hawkins said, smirking at the wordplay. "You don't see any value in this?"

"In torturing this man? Wasting my time and resources to watch over him? Not particularly."

"Dr. Loomis, you are a man of limited vision," Hawkins said. "If you knew Shane Ryan like I do—"

"I read the files you gave me," Dr. Loomis said.

"It's more than files. That's just the summation, the notes I bartered from the Cult of the Endless Night. It's nothing. To see him at work… Listen, I've followed this man's progress for years. I've seen him firsthand. He could have been at the top of the heap in this organization. The man can kill the dead with his bare goddamn hands, does that not mean anything to you? The power of death itself bows to his will. You think about that."

Dr. Loomis wanted his chair back, and to have a cup of tea and an apple, and to finish his notes. He did not want to listen to Brett Hawkins wax poetic while he made mountains out of molehills or acted like the bald, antisocial man locked in his hospital was some sort of cartoon hero.

"We need a plan, Mr. Hawkins," Dr. Loomis said. "Whether he commands the afterlife or sells newspapers is all the same to me. He can't just sit there forever."

Hawkins sighed and glanced around Dr. Loomis' sparse office.

"You seem like a dull guy, Doc," Hawkins said.

"Do I?"

"No art on your walls, no photos of the family. Do you have hobbies? Friends?"

"I have my work, Mr. Hawkins, which is what I'm trying to talk to you about."

"I have my work, too. That's what I *am* talking about. I could have gone my whole life without giving Shane Ryan another thought. I would have. I haven't seen him in person in years. Had I known Davis Blakely wanted to recruit him, I would have stopped him in his tracks. Had I known Ryan would go to Vakovia and do what he did, I would have diverted his flight. Hell, I would have crashed the plane. But this is where we are now. This is what we're dealing with."

Hawkins was frustrating to talk to. Dr. Loomis had patients amid psychotic breaks who were clearer and more forthcoming.

"Shane Ryan made a mess, Dr. Loomis. You see that, right?"

"I do," the doctor said.

"And I have been trying to clean up that mess. That's all that's happening."

"Do you want him dead?" Dr. Loomis asked bluntly. "That's all I need to do. I can make it look like an accident, self-inflicted, whatever fits your needs. I just need to know."

Hawkins scoffed.

"Limited, limited vision," Hawkins chided. "I don't want him dead, Dr. Loomis. I want to clean up the mess. If I wanted him dead, I would have splattered his brains across my kitchen when he broke into my goddamn house. I needed you because you have the skill to clean the mess."

"Mr. Hawkins…" Dr. Loomis began.

"Get rid of Shane Ryan. That's what I want. I need the rest of him. I need the body and the innate skills he possesses. I don't need the rest."

Dr. Loomis stared at Hawkins for a long moment, not sure he understood the man's meaning.

"What are you asking me to do, Mr. Hawkins?"

"Your job, Dr. Loomis. You have a dangerous patient who is unresponsive to treatment. You have determined that medication will not suffice, nor will any other traditional method of treatment. The only chance you have at offering this poor patient a chance at a normal life is a transorbital lobotomy."

The words hung heavily in the air. Both men held their silence for a moment, but Dr. Loomis could not help the smile that curled the corners of his lips.

"An interesting diagnosis I've developed," he said.

Dr. Loomis had only performed a lobotomy once before, and the patient had not survived. He was very young when he'd tried, and he had been a bit hasty in his preparation. The procedure was not sanctioned, of course, so he had to cut some corners. Even though the patient died, Dr. Loomis considered it a valuable learning experience. He had often thought he would like to have the chance to try it again.

"And what becomes of Mr. Ryan?"

"Assuming you perform the procedure well, which I'm sure you will?"

"Of course."

"Shane will be a valuable asset. No more problematic attitude means no more resistance. I want to make use of what Shane Ryan can do without the Shane Ryan part. If you cut that out, I can pop anyone else I want in there. I've got an entire roster of spectral assets that can do the job. They take the driver's seat, and we have our very own ghost-killing machine in the ranks. Is that clear enough, Doc?"

"Quite," Dr. Loomis said. "But I do wonder what the financial benefits are."

Hawkins laughed again.

"Of course, you do," he said. "I've already got interest from the Endless Night, from the Iron Tournament, and from others. This is a one-of-a-kind prize. A once-in-a-lifetime opportunity. You'll get paid handsomely, Dr. Loomis. Don't worry about that."

"Then it seems like we have a plan. If you'd told me that from the start—"

"You don't cook a steak until someone orders it, Dr. Loomis," Hawkins said. "That's why you need patience. That's why I waited until now to show up. And that's why you can go take Ryan and scrape his brain clean at your leisure. Just let me know when he's done and ready to travel."

Hawkins finally got out of the chair and left the room without another word. Dr. Loomis watched him go and, despite Hawkins' abrupt manner and frustrating method of doing business, Dr. Loomis found himself smiling.

He would get things ready for the procedure immediately.

CHAPTER 13
FIGHT FOR YOUR LIFE

No one came to give Shane his pills. That was his first indication that something was about to change. Jester had tried all day to come up with escape plans, but none of them were plausible or even realistic. Shane was still stuck in a straitjacket, and he was going nowhere without the use of his arms.

Meals were pushed through the slot under the door on schedule, and he wriggled over on the floor and ate as much as he could by pushing his face into it. It was undignified, but it was better than starving. Keeping up his strength was the most important thing he could do.

He wondered if Dr. Loomis had figured out that he wasn't taking his pills. Certainly, someone had realized Scarface was gone. Maybe they were recruiting a second ghost to come for him, or maybe they were going to ignore him. Bound as he was, alone as he was, Shane had a lot of time to go over potential scenarios.

The day dragged on. He could only discuss so many things with Jester. The ghost, in a much better mood than Shane had seen him so far, was still hard to talk to.

"We'll go together," Jester suggested.

"Sure," Shane agreed.

"In the basement. Keep me in the basement. Everyone in the basement."

"Jester, if you find a way to get me out of here, I will take you anywhere you need to go; you have my word," Shane said.

The wrinkled ghost nodded enthusiastically.

"Good deal," he said. "Good time to go."

Morning became afternoon became evening. As the light began to fade, Shane wondered if there would be any disturbance. Jester had not indicated there was another dangerous spirit around. It seemed unlikely to Shane. He bet that Dr. Loomis would leave him to rot until Hawkins came to finish the job or sent someone on his behalf. The man probably wouldn't want to get his hands dirty to disrupt his narrative of being Shane's doctor.

A key hit the lock in the door, and Shane raised an eyebrow. The tumblers rolled and clicked, and then the door pushed open. Dr. Loomis and Ephram came into the room together. The doctor held no tiny cups of pills, nor did he have his clipboard with him this time.

"Your visit today is later than usual," Shane said.

"Special occasion," Dr. Loomis answered. "I have something wonderful to show you, Shane."

Ephram punched him in the gut, and Shane doubled over. The big orderly stood behind Shane, grabbing a strap between his shoulder blades and forcing him to straighten up.

"Going for a walk in the garden?" Shane asked.

With Ephram behind him, he couldn't see the slap upside his head coming. The man's hand clapped over Shane's ear and made him wince as a ringing sound dulled his ability to hear for a moment.

"Much better, Shane. I'm going to perform a procedure that I think will make things a lot better for you. You're going to be a changed man."

Dr. Loomis left the room, and Ephram forced Shane to follow. The orderly held him at arm's length and directed him out of the room and to the left down the hall.

The doctor walked briskly and said nothing as they went through a set of security doors and took a left down another hallway. This part of the hospital was different from where they had come from. The rooms they passed were not patient rooms, they were operating rooms and offices.

Dr. Loomis entered a room, and Shane was forced to follow. A narrow aluminum table with restraints at wrist- and ankle-level made up the bulk of the room in the center. A light mounted on a bendable arm hung over it, and two small, movable trays of surgical instruments were on the far side of the table.

Shane said nothing as he kicked back as hard as he could, slamming his foot into Ephram's knee. He was barefoot, but he caught the orderly by surprise, and his heel hit at a good angle.

Ephram growled in pain and collapsed, but he did not let go of Shane. Instead, he dragged him to the ground with him, breaking one of the restraints. Shane kicked out again, hitting the orderly in the jaw. He struggled against the straitjacket and wound back for a third kick as Ephram grabbed the straitjacket and yanked Shane closer.

Seams tore, and Shane planted a foot into Ephram's groin. The larger man cursed and grabbed the jacket's collar. Shane pushed against him with both feet, and the top of the jacket burst. More seams popped, and his shoulders broke free.

Shane moved quickly, wriggling his body like a trapped animal. He got halfway out of the jacket before Ephram grabbed him, rolled him over, and slammed his face into the tile floor.

Spots danced before Shane's eyes, and his mouth filled with blood.

"Enough," Dr. Loomis said loudly. "If his face swells up too badly, I can't do the procedure."

Ephram grunted and lifted Shane like luggage. He hoisted him onto the aluminum table and pulled the straitjacket the rest of the way off, tossing it to one side.

Before Shane could react, the orderly strapped his ankles down tightly with the straps attached to the table. When he moved to wrap restraints around Shane's wrists, Shane spit blood into the man's face.

"You're awful at your job, you know that?" he taunted.

Ephram raised his fist, but Dr. Loomis put a hand on the man's bicep.

"Not the face," the doctor reiterated.

With a grunt, Ephram punched Shane in the gut, causing him to sputter more blood and groan.

"Man, you must be getting paid a good chunk of change for this, huh, Doctor?" Shane said, spitting again, this time on the table next to his head.

"Whatever do you mean, Shane?" Dr. Loomis asked.

The doctor was mostly ignoring Shane now, opting instead to select a few items from his tray. Shane had trouble seeing what he was handling, but there were flashes of silver. Dr. Loomis planned to perform surgery.

"Hawkins has deep pockets. Just wondering what it takes to make a doctor sell out these days. Assuming you are a real doctor."

"Of course, I'm a doctor," Dr. Loomis answered. "And I am doing this to help you, Shane. You are violent. You are sick. But you can get better. You can be happy and calm and a productive member of society again."

"That a fact?" Shane asked. He pulled at the restraints on his wrists and flexed his arms. "All I need to do is let you cut me up? Man, Hawkins lucked out when he found a lapdog like you."

Dr. Loomis smiled and sighed.

"I do my work because I have a passion for it, Shane. That's all that motivates me."

"Of course," Shane replied. The strap on his right hand pulled at his flesh as he tried to free himself. Ephram stood near the door, watching Shane with a surly expression.

"This is all you. You like to play pretend."

"Trying to goad me will not produce any results," Dr. Loomis said. "But I do understand why you would try."

"Of course, you do," Shane said. "Just like you understand why you let Big Boy over there do all your dirty work, just like you sent that useless scarred-up ghost. I destroyed him with my arms bound; that's embarrassing."

"There is no such thing as ghosts, Shane," Dr. Loomis said gently.

"Oh, I know," Shane replied. "Is this how you cope with everything? You have to lie to me; it's part of the gimmick. You lie to Ephram over there and tell him he's anything more than a thug? You lie to Hawkins and say you got me to take pills, and I didn't rip the throat out of your attack dog with my teeth?"

"Shane…" Dr. Loomis said.

"I know you're lying to yourself. You still think you're a doctor and not some midlevel stooge working for a disgraced former Marine captain who makes a living killing innocent civilians."

Dr. Loomis leaned over Shane.

"That's enough, Shane," he said calmly. He held a long, silver tool in his hand that looked like an ice pick with an old-style syringe handle. Shane recognized it, if not by name, then by purpose.

"This is a leucotome, Shane," the doctor said.

Shane kept the pressure on the cuff on his wrist. His hand was compressed as far as he could make it go, his missing fingers allowing him to compact the other digits into a much smaller space than normal.

"I'm going to slide the end in through the side of your eye socket, slipping around the eyeball until I reach the back of it. You have a thin layer of bone there that separates the eye from the frontal lobe of your brain," Dr. Loomis explained.

"A lobotomy?" Shane said, laughing in Dr. Loomis' face. "Seriously? The maddest procedure in the world. That's how you pretend you're a real doctor? My God, Dr. Loomis."

The doctor ignored him and continued.

"The bone will give way with enough pressure, and then, with a simple swishing gesture, the tip will sever the connection between your thalamus and prefrontal cortex. It will happen very quickly, so don't worry about spending all night strapped to the table."

"Yeah, big relief," Shane told him.

His arm was as tense as it could get. He felt the leather pulling and dragging at his flesh. It was not pulling away fast or easily enough. He lacked the leverage and angle. He needed time.

"So, what happens if you miss with that thing, Dr. Loomis?" Shane asked.

"Miss what?"

"My brain. You telling me you know how to use that tool? You've done this before?"

"Of course, Shane. I am a professional."

Shane laughed, rolling his eyes.

"How many people have you killed with one of those? I bet you have a closet full of skeletons."

"You have no idea what you're talking about," Dr. Loomis said. For the first time, Shane detected a different tone in the doctor's voice. Something was beyond the banal pleasantries now. There was frustration. Maybe even a hint of anger. Shane had found a loose thread. He needed to pull it.

"Oh, God. You murdered a patient," Shane said, grinning as obnoxiously as he could. "You Swiss-cheesed some poor schmuck's brain."

"I have never murdered anyone," Dr. Loomis countered coldly.

"Sure, yeah. And you never beat anyone; Ephram does it for you. Does Hawkins know you can't even do this procedure? Is he okay with you killing me? I bet you don't get paid if my brains leak out my nose."

He laughed again and Dr. Loomis leaned in close, the tip of the leucotome just a fraction of an inch from Shane's eye.

"I do not have to prove my skills to someone like you," Dr. Loomis said. "But I will when I slice your frontal lobe as cleanly as a butcher fileting a fish."

"A butcher fileting a fish?" Shane whispered, his eye fixed on the titanium point rather than Dr. Loomis' face. "That's grim as hell."

"It can get worse, Shane," Dr. Loomis said.

Shane smiled and glanced at the doctor's left hand gripping the base of the tool.

"It's about to."

He slipped his hand free of the leather shackle and snatched his hand out as fast as he could. Dr. Loomis did not see Shane move until he already had the leucotome in his grasp. In one swift, flowing movement, Shane took control of the tool and plunged it into the side of Dr. Loomis' head.

The titanium spike drove all the way into the doctor's temple. His left eye rolled back into his head as he collapsed, falling to the ground next to the aluminum table without a sound.

Shane reached for the restraint holding his other arm as Ephram rushed him. He would not have time to free himself, and his only weapon was lodged in Dr. Loomis' head on the floor.

He was out of options.

CHAPTER 14

INTO THE NIGHT

"You're a dead man," Ephram growled, speaking for the first time since Shane had met him. He was not bound by whatever deal Dr. Loomis had made with Hawkins. He would kill Shane without a second thought.

Three steps were all that separated the orderly from the table onto which he'd strapped Shane. He only made it to two.

Jester scuttled out from under the table and pulled Ephram's leg from under him. The orderly fell forward, smashing his head on the edge of the aluminum table with a dull thud.

Shane pulled at the other leather cuff that held him in place and then sat up to work on his ankles. He could see Ephram on the floor below, next to Dr. Loomis, a pool of blood slowly expanding around the bodies.

"Dead," Jester said, looking up at Shane and shrugging.

"Really?" Shane said. "Huh."

He freed his ankle and hopped off the table.

"Do you know the way out of here?" Shane asked.

"Out. Out and away," Jester answered, nodding.

Shane patted Dr. Loomis down, finding his wallet and keys and taking both.

"Basement first?" he asked.

The ghost grinned, and it made his wrinkled, jowly face look even more unpleasant.

"Basement," Jester agreed.

Shane had promised to take Jester with him, and he wasn't going to back out on the deal. Besides, he still needed Jester to get out of the building.

He stopped at the door and opened it a crack, peering down the hallway to see if anyone was coming. When he neither saw nor heard anything, he turned off the lights in the room and headed out, fumbling through several keys until Jester pointed out the right one to lock the door.

If Shane was lucky, Dr. Loomis hadn't told anyone where he was going. A lobotomy seemed like an unsanctioned procedure, so it was possible no one would know where to look for it. Shane would have some time before the bodies were discovered.

Jester let him down the hallway farther from the residence area where they'd started. A quick right turn, and they were at a door marked "Basement Storage". Shane unlocked the door and headed down into a cold, damp space.

The redheaded ghost with the wired jaw was at the base of the stairs as they descended. Others Shane recognized from the night before, when they attacked Scarface. He saw more that he did not recognize, some of them talking quietly among themselves as Shane approached.

"That way," Jester said, pointing ahead when they reached the bottom of the steps. They were in another hallway, this one made of old, red brick and concrete, with a trio of doors on either side.

They passed rooms full of files and another full of chairs and other office furniture before finding one labeled "Patient Effects". Shane had to unlock that door as well.

A rush of cold air swept over Shane's sock-covered feet when the door opened. The interior of the room was pitch black, but he didn't need lights to know there were ghosts inside. He could feel the fierce, unnatural cold like a winter storm was trapped within the confined space.

He found the light switch and clicked it on with a loud buzz. The room was full of plain shelves that held boxes of varying sizes. Each box had a number, a date, and a name with an initial. There had to be hundreds of them dating back decades.

To the left of the door, he found one labeled with his name, S. Ryan, and a reference number. His clothes were folded up inside, with his boots and a bag containing his wallet, cigarettes, keys, and lighter.

Jester scuttled off through the racks while other ghosts watched Shane take his belongings and get dressed in the doorway. He put the box with his hospital pajamas back on the shelf and then went in search of his companion.

"Here," Jester called from several rows back.

Ghosts whispered as Shane passed, but he could make out little of the conversation. Some of them looked aggressive, but they held back. His fight with Scarface might have made them think twice about pushing their luck, and he was happy to have them simply scowl from the shadows. He wanted to leave, nothing more.

Shane found Jester hunched low next to an open box. The label on the front was dated 1972. The name was H. Mitchum. He wondered if Jester was a Henry or a Harry.

More of the ghosts began whispering as Shane approached the box. Their numbers had increased, and he could see them watching intently from the shadows around the room.

"Fast," Jester said. "Fast, and it will be fine. Most have been here long. Longer than me."

"Are they all in these boxes?" Shane asked.

Having ghosts in a psychiatric hospital, especially an old one, was not surprising. But there were many in this place, and they were all in the same room that was as cold as an icebox. If most of the boxes held haunted items, the collection was intentional. And it predated Dr. Loomis if Jester had been there since the seventies. Someone was collecting the dead.

"Everyone. Everyone here," Jester confirmed. "Place for everyone. Everyone in their place."

Shane opened the box and looked at the contents. An old pair of moth-eaten corduroy pants, a pair of flattened loafers, and a silk shirt were on top. Shane pulled out an old bag of smaller items. The brittle plastic broke apart as he fished out a freezing cold pocketknife from a small pile of loose change, and some safety pins and buttons.

"This is old," Shane said, looking at the knife. The handle was a carved horn of some kind. Maybe an antler; it was hard to say. The blade was rusty and stiff.

"Dad gave it to me. Got it from Dad," Jester said, nodding and smiling at the knife.

Shane tore a strip from Jester's old pants, wrapped the knife in it, and then slipped it into his pocket. As he pushed the box back onto the shelf, he noticed a handful of empty slots on shelves where boxes had been slid out. Trails of dust gave an idea of how long they had been missing. Some had been recent; others probably had been taken months ago.

"Was Dr. Loomis the one taking boxes from here?" he asked, walking down the aisle. Just three boxes were missing, but the next aisle over had two missing, and the one after that was completely disheveled, with boxes scattered all over the floor.

"Don't know. Some. Maybe," Jester answered.

Shane walked to the messy aisle and realized what had happened when he found a box torn to pieces. It must have been Scarface's item. His destruction had scattered the nearby boxes on the shelves when the item broke.

"We should go now," Jester urged.

The murmuring of the nearby ghosts had grown louder. Some were creeping from the shadows in a way that reminded Shane of dogs or wolves warily approaching prey.

"Good thinking," Shane replied.

Jester shuffled away quickly, hunched low like an animal, while Shane weaved through the shelves back the way he'd come. The ghosts in the shadows were crowding closer and making their way toward the door. Shane cursed, wishing he'd left as soon as he'd found Jester's knife.

"Where do the ghosts they take out of here go?" Shane asked as they approached the door. He was trying to ignore the ghosts encroaching around him, even as their mumbles grew louder, and he could sense their agitation.

"Go away," Jester answered. "Take the stable ones away."

"Stable," Shane repeated.

"Sane. Take the sane. Take the rational."

The implication of who was left behind was not comforting. If Dr. Loomis was working with Hawkins and supplying him with spectral assets, then he would want to curate them. Ghosts that could be trusted to work with Reapers in the field were safe to recruit, but any who had died and retained their madness in the afterlife would not be. That was who crowded Shane now.

"So, Dr. Loomis was keeping tabs on you and the other ghosts?" Shane asked.

"They know. They all know. Watch and wait. He picked favorites, sent them away. He picked losers, kept them down. Scarface keeps them in line."

Jester did not seem concerned about the encroaching spirits despite his description of what happened in the basement. If it was Scarface's job to keep the other ghosts from getting out of hand, Shane had removed that concern. No wonder they were all so eager to join in destroying him. He had just handed the keys to the asylum to the inmates but had also locked himself in with them.

"Where are you going?" the ghost of a thin, blonde woman asked, stepping from behind one of the shelves between Shane and Jester. She spoke to the ghost and not to Shane, her intonation curious and disapproving.

"Away," Jester answered. "Gone and far, far and gone."

The woman turned to look at Shane. There were deep bruises around her throat as though someone had choked her. Her eyes narrowed.

"You're stealing him."

"He wanted to leave with me," Shane explained.

"You're stealing him," she said again. "You're stealing him!"

She began screaming, accusing him over and over again.

"Complication," Jester said over the sound of the screams.

"Stealing!"

The girl lashed out at Shane with an open-handed slap that caught him by surprise. His face snapped right, and the sting of the cold hurt more than the blow.

"Don't do that again," he told her.

"Stealing!"

Her hand raised a second time. He caught her by the wrist before she could follow through.

"You don't want to do that," Shane said gravely.

"Thief!" another of the spirits yelled.

"Kidnapper!"

More joined the chorus.

"We should go," Jester said.

Shane pushed the ghost who had slapped him away and followed Jester to the door. A second spirit, this one a man dressed in the ragged remains of a hospital gown, came at him from the shadows.

The ghost started to say something, but Shane planted an elbow into his face before he could voice a syllable. The ghost stumbled back, but the assault prompted more to attack.

"I'm just trying to leave," Shane said, punching another spirit in the jaw when it came for him.

They cursed him, spat, and screamed incoherently. They fed off each other's anger and pushed forward in a rush. Shane lost sight of Jester as ghostly hands pulled at his clothes and his flesh, yanking him this way and that while others beat at him or kicked him, trying to drag him to the ground.

Shane lashed out at anything and everything. He punched and kicked and tripped where and when he could, trying to break a hole in the assault long enough to get free or at least get a breather.

The redheaded ghost appeared in the mix as Shane was pulled to the ground. She stood over him, the wires in her mouth hanging out between her lips like thick, irregular hairs.

A fist hit Shane between the eyes, and another pummeled his kidneys. A foot came down on his neck, and he choked, scrambling to fight back with too many targets to choose from.

The redheaded ghost's lips parted. Her gums tore and blood gushed over her lips and down her chin as the most wretched scream Shane had ever heard filled the basement.

Ghosts covered their ears and shrank from the sound. Shane raised his hands, trying to drown out the noise that threatened to pierce his brain. It was like a drill boring into each ear, a sharp and fierce pain that seemed to go on and on.

He squeezed his eyes shut and gritted his teeth. The noise shook through them, vibrated into his bones, and twisted his insides.

When the sound finally subsided, Shane could still hear the echo like a living thing had taken up residence inside his skull. He opened his eyes and looked up at the ghost. Blood had saturated her, and wires hung loose from her face. She extended her hand.

Shane took it, and the ghost pulled him to his feet. She was shorter than him and when he was standing, she had to look up to maintain eye contact. She didn't speak a word, only stepped aside, and gestured to the door where Jester cowered, his ears still covered.

"Let's go," Shane said.

The wrinkled, old ghost did not need to be told twice.

CHAPTER 15
GETAWAY

Jester led Shane from the basement and back to the main floor. The hallways were dark and unused, whatever staff on hand was far away from them. Using Dr. Loomis' keys, Shane took them out a back door of the facility without anyone seeing or hearing a thing.

The sun had set, and the darkness helped cover their escape. It seemed no one had discovered Dr. Loomis or Ephram. Shane probably had until morning. He would have to make use of every minute. There was no way to know who else Dr. Loomis was working with, but he had to assume Hawkins would be informed quickly once the body was discovered.

Shane circled the building with Jester and stayed out of sight near some shrubs by the parking lot. A handful of cars were parked there, and Shane pressed the alarm button on Dr. Loomis' key fob to find the right vehicle.

"Long time," Jester said, huddled deep in the shrubs.

"For what?" Shane asked, looking for signs of night security.

"Long time since leaving. Long, long time."

"We should get going then. You've missed a lot since the seventies."

Ducking low and moving quickly, Shane made his way to Dr. Loomis' car and got in the driver's seat. The doctor drove a fire-engine red Tesla, not the most inconspicuous car in the world but better than nothing.

Jester was slow to follow but appeared in the backseat of the vehicle when Shane started it, huddled behind the passenger seat.

"Quiet," the ghost remarked.

"Makes getting away easier, I guess," Shane said, pulling out of the doctor's parking spot and putting the hospital behind them.

The GPS system on the car indicated they were in New York state, a rural area Shane wasn't familiar with. The hospital wasn't even on the map, and the GPS just showed the car lost in the wilderness.

"Where to now?" Jester asked, peering out the windows as Shane got onto an unlit forest road and headed east.

"Where do you want to go?" he replied. He had agreed to take Jester wherever he wanted, and the sooner he dropped off the ghost, the sooner he could get to Hawkins.

"Don't," Jester answered, staring out the window at the passing trees.

"Don't what?" Shane replied.

"Don't want to go."

He glanced over at the ghost and raised an eyebrow. Whether Jester knew it or not, they were on a timeline. Dr. Loomis' body would be discovered soon. His car could be tracked. The cops would be after Shane in a matter of hours.

"I have to take you somewhere," Shane told him.

"Where you go," the ghost answered.

"I've got things to do."

"I don't," Jester replied.

Shane sighed. He could just toss the knife out of the car and let the ghost haunt wherever he ended up. But Shane had made a promise to him, and Jester had saved his life.

"I'm going after the man who sent me to that hospital. The man who runs the Reapers."

"Captain Hawkins. Sure," Jester said. Shane had filled the ghost in on the pertinent details during his many long, drug-addled hours in the hospital. He wasn't sure what he'd said, but it had been enough.

"If you come with me, I'm going to need you to pull your weight, Jester. You'll need to fight."

"I fight," Jester said, nodding. He still had not taken his eyes off the window. "I kill."

Shane had not seen much evidence of Jester being an accomplished fighter, certainly not a killer, but he wasn't going to argue the point. If nothing else, the ghost knew how to stay out of the way. He could still potentially be useful for gathering information. Or just to watch Shane's back in a pinch.

"You don't have to do this," Shane told him. "It's not your fight. I can take you anywhere."

Jester grunted, his hands on the glass like a child while he watched the world pass by.

"Dead too long. Family's dead. World's not the same. Nowhere to go."

"Then why did you want me to help you escape?" Shane asked.

The ghost turned away from the window for a moment.

"Same reason you did. Never should have been there."

He turned back to the window and looked at the trees. Shane wondered if that was true. Had Jester been a sane and normal man? Maybe someone had placed him in the hospital to forget about him, too.

"All right, then," Shane said. "We're going to find Hawkins."

The hospital was about fifteen miles from the nearest town. It was close to midnight when they arrived, and the small town was as dead as the forest from which Shane had just appeared. With a population of just more than five hundred, there was little for anyone to do at that late hour, and Shane only saw two other cars on the road as he drove past the outskirts, looking for a place to stop.

The most brightly lit building in town was a gas station that, despite the lighting, wasn't open. Shane parked the Tesla around back where it wouldn't be seen right away and ventured out into the shadows.

"Find me something a little less obvious," Shane asked. "With keys, ideally."

He lit a cigarette next to the dumpster while Jester nodded, happy to have something to do, and shuffled off into the night. The town was deathly quiet, befitting the small size and location, but plenty of cars were parked in driveways. Surely, someone in small-town America was still foolish enough to leave their car unlocked.

Stealing cars from strangers was not something Shane had been comfortable doing, but it was an emergency. Since getting involved with the Reapers, he'd been forced to do far too many things he found distasteful. Hawkins had earned what he had coming and then some.

Shane finished his cigarette and Jester had yet to return. He stared at Dr. Loomis' Tesla and wondered what kind of tracking technology the thing had. Surely, the police could use the GPS to find it once they knew it had been stolen. Shane would be the obvious suspect.

There was an old pay phone on the side of the gas station wall. Shane glanced up and was happy to see no security cameras on the building, just lights. He picked up the receiver and dialed directory assistance.

Jester remained missing as Shane talked to the operator and placed a collect call. The hour was inconvenient, but he hoped James wouldn't mind.

"Hello?" James Moran said, the sound of sleep in his voice.

"Yeah, it's Shane. Sorry to wake you," he replied.

"No, it's fine I was just... yes, sleeping. It's fine. Are you still overseas? I heard some news..."

"No. I'm back. I'm in New York. Town called Brindle. I need a hand with something."

"Of course. Anything," James replied.

"It's going to bring heat down on someone, but I need the distraction, if you know someone who can get here soon."

He heard some rustling on the other end of the line.

"Brindle. Hmm. I have some contacts in Albany. I think I could have someone there within the hour, depending on the circumstances. This being a collect call, I assume something is wrong?"

"You could say that. I stole a car from a dead man. I need someone to keep driving the car, so the authorities track it thinking it's me."

"Did this man die of… natural causes?"

"He did not," Shane answered.

"Hmm," James intoned. There was another pause and some more shuffling.

"Where does the car need to go?"

"Back toward Nashua. They can ditch it before they're caught. I just need a few more hours. Whatever I can get."

"Okay. I can't promise my contacts will be willing to engage in a high-speed chase, but they can keep up the ruse for a time," James said, not sounding as confident as Shane would have liked.

"Like I said, whatever I can get is great. I appreciate it, James."

"Are you going to be safe, Shane? The news I heard from Vakovia was dire."

"I just escaped from a mental hospital where a doctor was trying to force a lobotomy on me," he answered.

"I see. Then you are probably eager to get going."

"I am," Shane answered. He gave James the address where his contact could find the Tesla and then thanked him for the assistance.

"I hope we can see each other soon under less intense circumstances," James said.

"Of course. Take care, James," Shane said before hanging up.

Jester was waiting at Shane's side when he finished. The ghost slinked silently out of the dark without Shane noticing and waited patiently for the call to end.

"Good. Good one. Come on," the ghost said. He slinked away, low to the ground, with his hands nearly dragging on the pavement.

Jester led Shane down the side of the gas station and up a quiet street full of dark houses.

"That one," Jester said, pointing to an old, gray Toyota in the driveway of a small bungalow. "See that one?"

"I see," Shane said, standing next to a tree out front of a house. The car was parked directly under a streetlight.

"Keys?"

"Right there. Ignition. Keys right there," Jester assured him. "Wait."

The ghost scurried off again toward the vehicle. Though his gait looked so awkward as to be painful, Jester was still very fast. He darted from the tree to the far side of the ride and then up the side of the pole that was planted out front of the house. The ghost's hand slipped into the housing of the streetlight, and the bulb hummed loudly before popping. The street fell into darkness.

Shane almost laughed as he slipped away from the tree and crossed over to the car. Jester dropped from the light pole alongside him and was in the car before Shane opened the door. This time, he'd chosen the front seat.

"Good. Good one," the ghost said, patting the dashboard.

The car smelled like cigarettes and fast food. The backseat was full of cardboard cups and hamburger wrappers, but the keys were in the ignition as the ghost had promised.

"Good one," Shane agreed. He started the car and pulled out of the driveway quickly, heading back to the main road.

The trip to Hawkins' home would take another two hours if he pushed the car as much as he dared. He couldn't get pulled over for speeding. He couldn't afford any run-ins with law enforcement until he reached his destination. He'd have to be cautious every step of the way.

If James followed through, then the Tesla would be on the road in an hour and heading in the opposite direction. It would give him breathing room and make Hawkins relax, at least a little.

Enough that he wouldn't be ready for Shane's arrival.

CHAPTER 16

MAKING MONSTERS

There was nothing Jester would not talk about. He remarked on houses and other cars and towns and trees. Miles and miles of mundane scenery fascinated him like nothing else. He pointed things out that Shane couldn't see in the dark and then added nothing else about them beyond acknowledging they existed. It grew tiresome very quickly.

Shane ignored the ghost and focused on driving, but it wasn't easy. Even when Shane refused to speak, Jester seemed to have no problem holding the conversation by himself.

"That fence is all stone," he'd said. "Maybe it's a wall."

"That car is old," he'd remarked right before saying, "that one isn't."

At best, he would get a grunt or nod out of Shane if he asked a specific question. They were rare, however, as the ghost was more intent on simply narrating his thoughts as they occurred in his head. It seemed like there was no filter between his brain and mouth.

"Why do you call yourself Jester?" Shane asked, trying to distract the ghost from describing the entire state of New York.

"Name," he replied.

"But who called you that? Seems more of a nickname for a comedian," Shane told him.

For the first time in quite a while, Jester grew quiet.

"Jester's my name," he said.

"Your box said H. Mitchum. That was your real name, right? You a Henry? Harold?"

With his jowls and wrinkles, either Henry or Harold would have suited him just fine. Maybe a Harvey, too.

"Jester," the ghost said quietly. "That's my name."

Shane glanced at the spirit, surprised by the quieter tone. He was no longer looking out the window and now focused on his hands in his lap.

"It's a good name," Shane said. "I'm not saying you need to change it."

"Hugo," Jester said eventually. "That was what they used to call me."

He was speaking in barely more than a whisper, as though he didn't want anyone to overhear what they were talking about. He stared at his hands and shook his head very slightly as though something there was disappointing him.

"Hugo Mitchum?" Shane asked.

Jester looked at him unsurely.

"Is that my name?"

"Is it?"

Jester raised his hands and held his head, leaning forward in his seat. He laced his fingers behind his skull and rocked gently back and forth.

Shane kept his eyes on the road, unsure of what he might have just unleashed in the ghost and hoping he wasn't going to regret it.

"If you want to stick with Jester, I'll stick with Jester," he assured the ghost.

"No... call me Hugo. My name is Hugo," he said, his head still down. "But had to be Jester."

Shane said nothing, keeping his eyes on the road.

"Dr. Zircher named me. Dr. Zircher's name."

"I don't know who that is," Shane said.

"He made us. Zircher makes monsters. He made us."

"What do you mean?"

The ghost's voice had gone very flat. Shane wished he could have convinced the spirit to speak more clearly, at least in full sentences. He had never heard of a Dr. Zircher, but if he was involved, Shane needed to know.

"Broke me. Had to break me. Small and stupid. Zircher said small and stupid. Dance like a clown. Jape like a jester."

"Is this Zircher still at the hospital?"

"Jape like a jester," Jester said again. "Broke me down. Can't dance with a broken back. Can't be a jester. Can't be alive."

He shook his head again and mumbled some words. Now Shane understood why the ghost was always scuttling, hunched and low to the ground. Though the spirit was not bound by earthly injuries, they still manifested in the ghost. Jester's broken back had been an intentional injury. It had left him crippled, and he carried it over to death.

"Wired Serena's mouth. Cut Scarface's face. Burned up Jackie Lantern. Monsters upon monsters," Jester said sadly.

Shane had thought Scarface had injured himself to manifest his many wounds. That a doctor had done that to him, Jester, the redheaded woman, and others was terrible. And to mock them after, to give him a name that made fun of his torment was something else. It was not the first doctor Shane had heard of who abused patients and created damned spirits that were dangerous and dark, but it was one of the cruelest.

"Maybe we can find Zircher someday, Hugo," Shane said. "If you want. If we survive."

"He's long gone," Hugo said. "Dr. Loomis was replacement."

"Retired doesn't mean dead," Shane said. "If he's still out there, we can find him. You can find anyone these days."

Hugo let his hands fall away from his face. He sat up as straight as his back would allow and looked back out the window.

"Half a century, isn't it?" Hugo said. "Been trapped there half a century."

"Time has a way of slipping through your fingers," Shane told him.

He knew ghosts who had been trapped much longer than Hugo. Even Eloise had been in the house on Berkley Street for more than a century;

Thaddeus as well. Carl would get there soon enough. Time didn't care about the dead.

"I wasn't good enough. Not viable. Not a viable product," Hugo said. "We need viable results. Functional. Need to be functional."

"Zircher said that?" Shane asked.

"Scarface too unpredictable. Serena too timid. Not viable."

It sounded to Shane as though Zircher had tried to curate ghosts. Dr. Loomis working with Hawkins was no coincidence if he had taken over from a man like that. Dr. Loomis, and Zircher before him, were essentially arms dealers.

The Reapers didn't date back to the seventies, but that didn't mean anything. It wouldn't surprise Shane to learn that Hawkins wasn't creative enough to come up with the idea. There was a market for ghosts. The Endless Night collected them. Men like Guthrie bought them for the Iron Tournament.

Hunting them naturally was time-consuming and dangerous. Most ghosts didn't want to be found, and many that would have been desirable to people like Hawkins would have been well set in their ways. Old, dangerous, powerful, and unpredictable. Farming them would have been a much better solution.

Shane could only imagine how long. How long had people been cultivating the dead? How long had they been trying to force a ghost out of a living person? One that would be powerful but controllable. One that would be terrifying but reliable. And not just one, but many. An army.

As far as Shane knew, there was no safe way to build a ghost. They weren't robots that could be assembled and programmed. Death was not a canvas on which an artist could paint.

Even the most perfect idea of a soldier in life could become something unexpected in death. Eloise had just been a little girl. Death had made her calculating, even cold sometimes. But a child at others.

Things like Scarface should have proven that there were flaws in the idea of forcing a ghost to exist. If some came back as spirits and seemed moldable, it could have just as easily been an act. Hawkins was sitting on a powder keg if that was how he outfitted the Reapers.

Shane could hardly comprehend the inhumanity. Humans being cruel to other humans was not a surprise. He had been a Marine for too long to be surprised by the suffering one person could bring upon another. But there was more to making a ghost than just killing a person.

Not everyone came back from the dead. There didn't seem to be any rhyme or reason to it. It wasn't half or a third or a tenth. There was no formula. Some of the dead stayed dead. Some didn't.

If Dr. Loomis and his predecessor had tried to force the creation of ghosts, they would have needlessly killed dozens, if not hundreds. Shane wondered where they came from. They couldn't have all been patients. They'd be unreliable from the start. A person with a psychiatric disorder who was tortured and murdered would be unpredictable in death.

The answer was obvious, of course. They weren't real psychiatric patients. Shane hadn't been one, but it was easy enough for Dr. Loomis to convince the FBI he was. How easy would it have been for him or Zircher to do the same to innocent people ten or twenty or fifty years earlier?

"How did you end up in that hospital, Hugo?"

"Oh, they found me," he answered as if that explained anything.

"Zircher?"

"Found me in Buffalo, don't ya know? Down in Buffalo. Cold night. Needed a bed. Needed a meal."

"You were on the street?"

"Cold," Hugo said, nodding. "Cold on the street. Cold and hungry."

"So, they promised you a place to eat and sleep and then kept you there?"

"Good trick, huh?" Hugo said, chuckling. "Jester wasn't a bad name for a fool."

Shane left Hugo to enjoy the view out of the window for the last few miles of their journey. They were getting close to Hawkins' house, and they would need a plan to approach the place.

There were too many ghosts on site for Shane's liking, but with Hugo's help, he could think up a distraction. He'd have to. He had the basic layout of the house in his head and knew how to navigate around once he got inside. If Hawkins wasn't expecting him, then Shane could find him quickly, ideally before the man set off an alarm.

A lot was left up to chance. Dr. Loomis was still a ticking clock, so Shane had to come up with a plan on the fly. He didn't like working under that kind of pressure, but the upside was that Hawkins was just as unprepared. At least Shane knew what was coming. He had that edge.

Shane knew to avoid the quiet, rural street on which Hawkins' house was situated. The landscape was too open, and a car driving past at night would be noted by the ghost guards and many cameras. They needed a stealthier approach.

The house was surrounded by a forest, and Shane planned to make his way in from the back. When he was within several miles of Hawkins' home, he caught sight of a sign for the local dump and headed that way.

"We need to ditch this car, maybe improvise some supplies," Shane explained to Hugo.

Like Hawkins' house, the dump was not in the town. It was a few miles from civilization and coupled with auto wreckers.

"Think you can get the cameras, locks, and lights?" Shane asked, pulling off the road near the gates to the wreckers. Hugo stared out the window at the sprawling lot full of iron and steel beyond the barbed-wire-topped fences.

"Used to work at a place like this in the fifties," he said. No other answer was forthcoming. He left the car and vanished into the night.

Minutes passed while Shane idled by the side of the road. One of the large tower lights illuminating the scrap lot flickered and went dead. A moment later, the same happened to the next light, and then the next. The smaller lights in the office buzzed out as well. Soon, the entire lot was in darkness, and Shane crept up to the gate.

The padlock holding the chain at the gate fell away as Hugo emerged from the darkness.

"Good. Good to go," he said, as Shane got out of the car to push open the gate.

"Let it never be said you're not good at what you do, Hugo," Shane said, getting back into the car.

He drove slowly onto the lot and past the office, into the depths of the junkyard until he found a suitable spot to ditch the vehicle where he hoped it'd go unnoticed for a time.

"Now what?" Hugo asked.

"Now, we improvise," Shane said, looking at the piles of trash around them. There were a thousand and one ways to take out a ghost with items in a scrapyard. And ten times as many to use against a living man.

CHAPTER 17
INFILTRATION

"How do you hurt them?" Hugo asked as Shane picked through a pile of scrap metal. They were searching through piles of metal housed in a ramshackle workshop located in a shed. The owner of the scrapyard clearly used the place to break things down, maybe to retrieve usable parts or for ease of recycling. Whatever the case, the covered room had several saws and grinders as well as bins and bins of scrap.

"Hurt who?"

"The dead. Scarface."

"Something I've been able to do for a long time," Shane told him. "You're all real to me. Physical."

"Maybe not," the ghost replied.

Shane pulled a metal rod from a pile and held it up. Hugo reached for it and laid a hand on it.

"Not iron."

Shane grunted and tossed it aside.

"What do you mean maybe not?" he asked.

"Maybe we're not real to you."

"I can touch you. Any ghost," Shane said. Maybe he needed to choose a better word for Hugo to understand.

"No. Maybe you real to us."

Shane stopped rifling through the metal and looked at the wrinkled face next to his.

"Now what do you mean?" he asked.

"You ever die?"

"Almost," Shane said. "More than once."

"But so close. Ever die that much? Maybe it came back with you."

"What came back? Death?"

"Maybe," Hugo said. "That's what we are. Body was life. It was born. It grew. It died. This is death. This is what came after."

Shane had considered this. The link between himself and the spirit world was undeniable. But the meaning or even any potential reason, was not something he wanted to concern himself with. Did it matter? Carl was more interested in philosophy than Shane; he'd leave it to him to ponder.

"Maybe, Hugo," Shane said. He pulled another length of metal, long and thin like a baton, and held it up. Hugo reached for it and vanished in a blink, appearing a moment later like he had glitched out of reality and then back into it.

"Iron," he confirmed.

Shane kept the rod and moved from the scrap heap to some large cans of rusted bits and filings. Some held old bolts and nuts, others were just mismatched chunks that had been cut or torn from metal items.

At the base of the largest grinder was a long, flat bin full of the smallest filings. Gravel-sized bits of metal, many of them twisted into tiny corkscrews or ground down into flecks. Shane picked up a handful.

"Try this," he said.

Hugo plunged his hand into the bin and popped again.

"Not all iron. But some," he said.

It would be good enough. He scanned the walls of the shed and found some small jars that had been used to collect screws of various sizes. Shane dumped them out, scooped up the filings, sealed the jars, and dropped a couple into each pocket.

"How much time?" Hugo asked.

"No idea," Shane replied honestly. Had Dr. Loomis been discovered? Or the Tesla? They had to get moving, regardless. "Let's go."

Hugo proved to be a reliable navigator as they fled the scrapyard and headed into the woods. He cut a line through the forest directly toward where Shane had told him the house was located.

The ghost ran from tree to tree, still hunched over, pausing when he needed Shane to catch up, and then leading the way again. The distance passed in swift silence, and Shane neither saw nor heard anything until they reached the forest's edge.

Hawkins' house was much the same as it had been on his first pass. Ghosts wandered the ground, but there were fewer this time. The ones he saw before must have been there in anticipation of his arrival. There were only three now.

Shane and Hugo crouched in the underbrush near the edge of the woods and watched their movements. They were doing a simple patrol, but one that did not leave many openings.

Human sentries might have been easier to dupe in the darkness, but ghosts had excellent vision. It would be nearly impossible for Shane to get close without at least one of them seeing him. Not to mention the cameras that still dotted the house at regular intervals and covered the property.

"Tough. Tough run," Hugo said.

"Yeah. Can't go directly; they'll set off an alarm. We need a back door," Shane said.

If Hawkins operated Reaper Company from the house, there had to be more to it than met the eye. A secret office, an underground facility, or something.

Hawkins' family lived in the home, or at least he wanted it to look that way. There was no way he had ghost mercenaries stored a room away from his children and grandchildren, especially if some of the recruits came from a psych facility. Hawkins was greedy, but he wasn't an idiot.

"There's no way Hawkins just lives in a haunted house," Shane said. "There's something we're not seeing."

"Down," Hugo said, pointing to the far right.

Shane followed with his eyes as best as he could. There was something small sticking out of the ground in the yard behind the house. It was hard to make out in the poor light, but it looked like a simple column of some kind, just a couple of feet tall.

"That's a vent," he said. The metal column curved slightly at the top and must have had an outward-facing grate to allow airflow but not rain to enter. There was something underground, and it needed airflow.

"Go see what you can find. But don't let them see you," Shane said.

"Like a ghost," Hugo said, and Shane was not sure if it was meant to be a joke.

Hugo vanished into the earth and Shane stayed hidden, watching the sentries do their patrol. If Hugo was discovered, Shane expected some sort of disruption to the routine of the guards. He could leave and once he was far enough away, he could take Hugo with him if it came to that, thanks to the knife in his pocket.

The ghost guards continued their circuit around the house. Once, twice, three times. Their pace never changed, nor did anything else. Shane watched the darkness in case Hugo or anyone else showed up unexpectedly.

It became a hypnotic sort of drudgery. The guards seemed to walk in their own footsteps like an endless funeral procession, again and again, going nowhere. The ghosts never tired, and they never needed to waver from their path unless something caught their attention.

Shane wondered if there was a limit to what a ghost could do. They never grew tired, but was that limitless? Could Hawkins keep these spirits wandering around his house for years on end? If a ghost was set to a task, would it keep going until the end of time?

Eloise was the most unsettled of the spirits at Shane's house. She had been trapped in the walls for more than a century, and he wondered what that implied for the future. He often fell into the trap of thinking about things in terms of his lifetime. A long time for a living man might be seventy years. But what was a long time to Eloise?

The day would come when Shane was no longer around. Even if he lived to a ripe old age, Eloise would be the same little girl. Though her flesh was desiccated, her hair was dry and stringy, and the scent of rot followed in her wake, she was still the same child she had been when she died more than a hundred years before. What would happen in the next hundred years? What would happen in five hundred years?

It was hard to perceive the reality of eternity. Shane didn't know if that's what ghosts had to look forward to. If these ghosts could wander around Hawkins' house without stopping, if Eloise could wander the walls for a hundred years, was there anything outside of Shane that could put an end to their existence?

The prospect of eternity was more terrifying than any ghost Shane had encountered. He wondered if perhaps that was part of what twisted a soul when the living body died and the spirit remained. Did they glimpse what was coming for them and lose their humanity? Was knowing that you might exist forever, trapped in one place and unable to grow, something any mind could understand and accept?

Hugo returned then, soundlessly appearing at Shane's side in the weeds and tree cover.

"It's there. Down there," he said.

"What is?" Shane asked, pushing the other thoughts from his mind.

"Military. Like a base. Looks official."

"Personnel?" Shane asked.

"Personnel?" Hugo responded with a perplexed look on his face.

"How many people are down there?"

"Some. Ghosts. Not sure."

It was not the best answer, but better that Hugo didn't get caught trying to count heads. If it was large enough to require air vents, Hawkins probably had a secondary entrance. The house couldn't be the only way to gain access.

"Now I just need a way in," Shane said more to himself than the ghost.

"There's an entrance," Hugo said. "Different entrance."

"Where?"

"Far. Tunnel west. A garage."

Hugo pointed again, in the same direction as the air vent, but toward something that was not visible from where they were. They would have to travel through the woods again, but Hugo assured him the tunnel came out on a neighboring property.

Shane and the ghost tucked back behind the tree line, away from the view of the ghost guards, and ran toward the garage. Hugo led the way again, confident in his navigational skills. They circled wide of Hawkins' property and came out into the yard of a second house that Shane had not seen on his previous visit.

The house was in the distance, just off a road that Shane had not traveled. There were no lights on, and the garage in the back was unguarded. It was an older and inconspicuous-looking building. The exterior was wood paneling with no windows, and the brown paint was flat and chipped in many places. Several security cameras hung from the corners of the building and covered the surrounding area.

Hugo approached the garage and shorted out the security cameras, forcing his hands into the casing and causing a quick spark and puff of smoke to come out of each one. When he finished, he waved Shane over.

Nothing about the garage looked suspicious from the outside. The rest of the property appeared to be a regular house in the country, if somewhat less ostentatious than Hawkins' house.

The property needed some maintenance; no one had mowed the lawn recently. Shane would not have given anything a second glance if he had driven by.

He tried the door to the garage and found it locked. Hugo passed through the wall, and the locked door clicked a moment later.

Shane entered into a dark space, but an overhead light clicked on immediately, triggered by a motion sensor. The single light illuminated an empty room save for a single door in the middle of the garage. It was mounted inside a cement frame that vanished into the ground, creating a triangle of plain, white concrete with the simple gray door mounted on the outward-facing side.

Hugo passed through the door, and then quickly returned.

"Empty. Safe place," the ghost said.

Shane pulled open the door and looked down a set of metal stairs that descended into darkness. If anything was there, Hugo would have seen. He had to trust that his companion was looking out for him.

"Let's go see what Hawkins is hiding in the dark," Shane said.

CHAPTER 18
WHAT LIES BENEATH

Shadows danced in the flickering flames of Shane's lighter. The metal stairs in the garage led down to a plain, concrete tunnel. It reminded Shane of access tunnels he'd seen in subways and sewers. Unadorned and simple, cold, and quiet. There was only one direction to walk, so he and Hugo headed forward into the darkness.

The concrete made his footsteps echo, but he could do little to avoid it. His lighter only illuminated a small area, but Hugo could see farther and said there was nothing ahead.

If the tunnel went straight back to the facility that Hugo had found under Hawkins' house, then they had perhaps half a mile to walk before anything changed. That also meant there was nowhere Shane could run or hide if a trap had been set up along the way to prevent people from snooping.

He saw no sign of security cameras in the tunnel, but there were regularly placed lights in the ceiling that must have had a control somewhere. It was just as well to travel by the flame of the lighter to not give away that he was there.

Hugo kept silent on their walk, a stark change of pace for the ghost who was normally very chatty when it was just the two of them. Quirky though Hugo might have been, he understood the situation.

Shane moved briskly, but not so fast that his footfalls were loud enough to draw attention. He kept his eye out for any variation along the path that might indicate a doorway or some other passage, but nothing revealed itself.

"It's dark," Hugo said, looking ahead. "Too dark."

Shane held up the lighter, extending his arm as far as it could go to increase the reach. Nothing looked different to him about the path ahead, but Hugo had slowed considerably.

"Something there?" he asked.

"Just dark. Can't see."

Ghosts could see very well in the dark. The only time a ghost couldn't see was when something was intentionally hidden. Shadows created by another ghost, for instance. Those could be impenetrable.

Shane kept walking, not wanting to give away his suspicions. There was no place else to go, anyway. He matched Hugo's slower pace until he saw that the light from the Zippo was growing smaller.

"I'll check," Hugo suggested.

"No," Shane said. "I will."

He walked until his feet were at the edge of the shadow that refused to move. His toes were inches away from it, and he stared into a void that refused to show itself, despite the lighter he held above his head.

"Hello," he whispered, lowering his hand. "Going to need you to move."

Shane reached into the darkness with his free hand. It felt like reaching into a freezer. The cold air rolled across his fingertips and circled his knuckles. There was nothing but empty space, but Shane's hand vanished just inches in front of his face.

Something brushed against the side of Shane's hand. He resisted the instinct to pull away and instead slowly swept his hand from side to side.

The thing in the dark brushed against him again, and this time he felt a crisp, biting cold. He kept his face calm and his expression blank. One more pass with his hand in the dark, a wide arch sweeping back and forth, and finally, the hidden thing stopped him.

Something took hold of his hand. Shane waited for an instant and then returned the favor. He closed his fingers around something solid and cold like ice. He dropped the Zippo from his other hand and reached into the blackness.

His hands held firm as he pulled forward, leaning back with all of his weight. The wall of shadow collapsed, and the light from the small flame filled the space, casting new, flickering shadows on the empty tunnel.

A figure stumbled toward Shane, clutched in his hands, and struggled to get free. Shane could see the poor light reflected in wide, damp eyes. A mouthful of twisted and missing teeth snapped at his face, and he fell all the way back, dragging the ghost to the ground with him.

The tunnel guard was not one of the spirits that Hawkins had used around his house. Shane rolled and fought with the thing on the ground, trying to keep hold of the arm he had pulled from the shadow while the ghost snapped at him and dug at his legs with gnarled and bony feet.

The ghost bucked and writhed. Shane could barely focus on what he saw. He thought it was a man, but identifying such features was not his chief concern. It was thin and bony, emaciated as much as any corpse he had ever seen. The hairless body was smooth and slick like it had been oiled, and Shane had a hard time keeping a grip on it.

Strained, breathy noises came from it, grunts and chuffs. It sounded like noises from a person choking.

The arm slipped from Shane's grip, and he was forced to embrace the spirit's torso, rolling on top of the squirming mass, and pinning it down. It sank teeth into the side of his jaw, biting just below his cheek, but Hugo struck the ghost with a quick punch to the top of its bare head before it could cause serious damage.

The ghost growled and head-butted Shane in the face. The blow caught him by surprise, the strength of it making spots dance in his eyes. It was only a momentary distraction, but the spirit capitalized on it and vanished, leaving Shane on the ground holding his face.

"Gone," Hugo said, looking around. "Fast."

"We can't let him warn Hawkins," Shane said, grabbing his lighter and getting to his feet. He ran down the hallway, knowing the exit had to be close and hoping to find the ghost in time.

"Go ahead and see if you can track him," Shane said.

When Hugo didn't answer, Shane turned to look back and stopped dead in his tracks.

The space behind Shane was no longer the empty tunnel through which he had walked. In the light of the Zippo, it looked like a vast, empty plateau. The cement extended as far as he could see in every direction before the shadows swallowed it. The tunnel was gone, and he was alone in the dark.

"Hugo?" he called out.

His companion had vanished with the tunnel. Shane cursed and turned in a circle, holding the lighter high, and feeling it grow warmer by the second.

What he was seeing was not real. The ghost was showing him an illusion, something his mind could not see through. But knowing it was not real did nothing to help him escape. A ghostly illusion could be deadly if it couldn't be overcome.

The air was still and stagnant. There was a faint odor around him like something had died there a long time ago. Or maybe there was a bog in the distance, too far to see but not too far to offend the senses.

Shane walked in what he thought was a straight line. He knew the illusion could make him spin in circles and not realize he was going nowhere.

It was frustrating to be caught in a ghost trap, and the danger was very real. But there was an upside. The ghost had chosen to stay to trick him. It was going to try to kill him, Shane had no doubt. That meant it was not going to warn Hawkins.

Shane continued walking, listening, and watching for evidence of anything in the darkness. Something clattered, a blunt and muffled sound. He turned in a circle and caught the very edge of a shadow moving at eye level, up and out of sight.

The light from the Zippo only penetrated so far. Shane strained to see something, anything, but he could not even make out a shape.

There was a sudden gust of wind, and the flame flattened and shuddered, struggling to stay lit. A soft, breathy laugh echoed across the vast emptiness. The lighter went out.

Shane was swallowed by the shadows. He flicked the wheel of the lighter but couldn't make a spark. After a second try elicited the same results, he gave up and slipped the warm metal back into his pocket. Best to have both hands free.

He could hear the laughter again, and it sounded closer. It was not a robust laugh, nor manic in any way. It was a soft, tired laugh, and the sound was almost soothing.

Walking was a risk. The darkness was too thick and all-encompassing. Shane couldn't even see his hand in front of his face. Without knowing the lay of the land, he could fall into a hole and break his neck if he took another step. Instead, he waited.

The stagnant smell grew thicker. It was all mildew, rot, and the stink of things that never saw sunlight. It came to his nose on a cold, slow breeze.

"I want you…"

The voice was impossibly quiet. It was a muffled whisper, a reluctant admission stifled by a wall, a pillow, or a fist. Shane puzzled over the words for a moment in the darkness.

"…to bleed."

The final syllable hit harder. It was spoken in a sob, as though the ghost did not want to admit its desires and felt shame for them. Shane said nothing. He would not play the game.

"I want you to scream."

The voice was closer now, its tone apologetic. There was nothing to see, and Shane knew trying to track the sound would prove fruitless. The ghost was not giving itself away so easily.

"I want you to die."

The words were whispered directly into Shane's ear. The stench of rotten things rolled over him. He didn't hesitate.

Shane's elbow took the ghost in the jaw as he spun to the right. He caught the spirit with his left hand before it could fall, and then pulled it close.

The illusion crumbled around him, and Shane was back in the tunnel. Little had changed that he could see in the dark, but he could feel the tunnel walls again.

"You first," Shane said, grasping the ghost's head in his hands. He forced it to the ground as it struggled and gasped, trying to break away.

Shane dug in his fingers and felt his muscles tense. He strained and squeezed, bringing his hands together. The flesh of the spirit gave way and crushed inward. It pushed back on him in the next instant as the explosion spread in all directions. Shane was thrown back and landed looking up at nothing as the expulsion of energy washed over him.

CHAPTER 19

INTO THE PIT

"Not dead."

Shane could vaguely make out Hugo's face looking down at him.

"Not in so many words," he agreed.

"Thought you might be."

"Takes more than that," Shane said, sitting up. The tunnel was still silent. No indication that anyone had heard the blast from the spirit's destruction.

"Rest of the way is clear. Good path," Hugo told him.

Shane got to his feet, dusting himself off and straightening his clothes.

"You ran ahead to find the path while I was dealing with that?"

"Sure," Hugo said. "Seemed like a good idea."

The ghost led the way through the dark to the end of the line without any further interruptions. The tunnel ended in another door identical to the one they had used to enter the tunnel in the garage. Hugo manipulated the lock, and the door popped open, revealing bright, fluorescent lights that made Shane squint.

The space looked like an office building designed for efficiency rather than aesthetics. The tile and paint had a green cast, and the humming lights overhead picked up on it, giving the hallway a sickly hue.

Shane pulled the door closed behind him and stared down a long, empty hall that ended in another door, this one with a complex latching mechanism. Rooms lined this new hall on either side, each windowless and labeled with only numbers. The exit was 166. The next door to his left was 165.

"Big place," Shane said, assuming the numbers were sequential.

"Large," Hugo agreed. "But mostly empty."

Shane took a look inside 165. It held cleaning supplies. There were shelves of cleansers, degreasers, bleach, and soap. Others were piled with paper towels and sponges. It looked like something fit for a large office building that catered to hundreds of people. It made him wonder what Hawkins was doing down there.

Shane found wiring in room 164. There were huge wheels of cable, bins full of phone and USB dongles, random adapters, ethernet cables, HDMI cords, and more. It looked like an electronics surplus store.

"The hell is all of this for?" he said quietly.

"Bunker," Hugo said. "Walls are concrete. Six feet maybe. Looks like a bunker."

Hawkins had designed a large-scale panic room for himself, then, but one from which he planned to still run things if some sort of cataclysm happened. The fact he was farming mercenaries and dabbling in assassinations and world politics made the whole thing more ominous.

It seemed like Hawkins was aware that Reaper Company could end up pushing countries toward war, and that maybe, the U.S. would be held responsible. And his solution was to build a bunker to hide in, just in case.

They ignored the rest of the rooms in the hallway that Shane was certain were just additional storage places and reached the next unmarked door. Shane laid his hand on it and felt the heft of the metal.

"Is this lead?" he asked.

Huge pressed his hand against the door and could not pass through it.

"Yes," he said.

Lead could hold spirits as easily as the living. It was an impenetrable prison for them, but that was not the reason for the door. The walls around it were not lead; they were concrete. Hawkins was not trying to keep ghosts out or in. The door was meant to shield someone from a nuclear blast.

Shane grabbed hold of the handle, a large, spoked wheel in the center of the door, and spun the mechanism to the right. He could hear the tumblers in the door rumbling as the locking pins retracted. Eventually, the door fell open to reveal what waited on the opposite side.

Beyond the blast door was a shallow vestibule. That gave way to a room that housed a handful of ghosts that didn't see him in the doorway. He ducked behind the door frame, hidden by the thickness of the opened blast door, and peered in.

Basic tables and chairs were set up in the room, and the ceiling was higher than in the hallway. Four ghosts stood together in the farthest corner of the room, the only corner Shane could see, talking among themselves.

"Looks bad," Hugo whispered, watching the spirits with Shane.

He had never seen them before, but he had no doubt they were spectral assets. The tallest of the ghosts was skinned to the waist, his body glistening with blood that dripped slowly over the exposed tissue. Below the waist, he still wore camo pants and standard-issue boots, and both were soaked and red.

Opposite the fleshless spirit, a dark-haired woman covered in stab wounds spoke to the group, her voice too soft for Shane to hear. She faced a short, wide monster of a ghost that was covered in coarse body hair whose entire lower body was burned black.

The fourth member of the group was bloated and decayed, thick with rot, and dribbling brown water that pooled at its feet but faded from existence before it traveled too far.

"Looks like horror movie tryouts," Shane said.

He knew the Reapers prized skill, but there were some points for appearance. A ghost that looked terrifying could do more damage than one that looked like an accountant, at least psychologically.

Other ghosts passed by the door, and Shane pressed himself tight to the wall, staying out of sight as best as he could. It looked like they were socializing in some kind of common area. Hawkins had created a barracks for his spectral assets, a place to relax in their downtime. He wondered how many were down there.

"We need a way through," Shane whispered to Hugo.

"I can blend in," the ghost suggested.

Shane shook his head.

"They'll know you don't belong."

They needed to find a way to distract them or get them to go somewhere else without raising too many suspicions.

"Yo!"

The shout came from inside the room and Shane froze, balling his hands into fists.

"Control room in five," the voice shouted before the sound of a door clicking ended the announcement.

Shane remained with his back to the wall, hidden by the edge of the blast door. He heard a smattering of voices and then another door clicking. Conversations grew faint, and finally, a door closing led to silence.

He glanced at Hugo huddled next to him. The ghost tentatively peered around the corner.

"Gone," he whispered, stepping out and exposing himself. "Everyone gone."

"Hold up," Shane cautioned before the ghost went too far.

He looked out as well and confirmed the four ghosts from the corner had left. He crept forward, crossing the threshold of the door, and entering the small vestibule. Carefully, he sneaked a glance around the corner.

The room was not as large as he expected it to be. It was closer in size to a family rec room that maybe took up the basement floor of an average house. There were a handful of tables and chairs, and some sofas along the far wall. There was even a television. But no ghosts remained.

Four other doors led out of the room, two of them blast doors and two not. Shane had a hard time understanding what the hell Hawkins had created or why. The common room, with the ghosts just hanging out, made him think of a military base, albeit a makeshift one. But all the storage rooms contained items that would only be of use to the living.

He entered the room and strode across the floor to the door on the opposite wall, the one he saw others use to exit the room.

"It's got to be four in the morning," Shane said quietly. "Who calls a meeting at four in the morning?"

"Ghosts," Hugo offered.

There was something to be said for the dead operating differently than the living, but Shane didn't like the way it felt. Part of him feared they had discovered Dr. Loomis, but if they had, there would be more urgency. Maybe something else was at hand. A new mission for the Reapers. Maybe they were about to be deployed.

Shane waited at the door, listening intently. There were no sounds of conversation and no movement from the other side. He grabbed the handle and pushed the door open into a new hallway. A click from behind stopped him from taking a step.

"Oh," Hugo said softly.

Shane turned to look back the way they had come. The fleshless ghost and the stabbed woman stood on either side of Alex Patton. Both ghosts watched Hugo, ready to take on the spirit if he made a move. Patton, of course, only had eyes for Shane.

"Ryan, what the hell are you doing here?" the lieutenant asked. He held his arm outstretched, the barrel of his M18 pistol pointed at Shane's head.

He was as still as stone, and Shane had no doubt that the man would have no qualms about killing him on the spot. There had been more than one reason he'd never liked Patton.

"Being held at gunpoint, it would seem," he replied.

"Hands," Patton said.

Shane complied and raised his hands to head level, palms inward.

Patton looked him up and down quickly and laughed. It was the same derisive, bully laugh Shane remembered from Afghanistan, the sort of mocking laugh you'd expect to hear in a schoolyard when a bigger kid finds a way to make a weaker one feel bad.

"God, you're not even armed, are you? You broke in here with no weapon and, what, an elderly hunchback?"

He gestured haphazardly at Hugo, and Shane shrugged.

"You don't use a rocket launcher to swat a mosquito," Shane told him. Patton laughed again.

"You always had quips, didn't you? Real quippy guy. Say something quippy to convince me not to blow your brains all over the wall."

Shane smiled at Patton. He couldn't cross the distance in the time it would take to get to him before Patton could pull the trigger. He was an asshole, but he was efficient and decisive, and he always had been. He would shoot Shane if given cause. But he didn't have cause yet, and that meant something.

"You're not allowed," Shane answered simply.

"What?"

"If you were allowed to kill me, you would have done it the first time I saw you. Hell, the second time. You don't have permission, Alex."

With his hands still up, Shane dropped the majority of his fingers, flipping Patton off with both hands. Patton's nostrils flared, and Shane watched his hand tense on the gun. He wanted to pull the trigger, but they hadn't wasted time getting him committed just to kill him outright. Hawkins wanted him, and Patton knew it. Shane would live so long as he didn't force the issue and give Patton an excuse to claim he had to do it.

"When you die, Ryan, I'm going to be the one to pull the trigger."

"That's the spirit, tiger. You reach for those stars," Shane snickered.

The lieutenant adjusted the grip on his gun and took a step forward, pulling the hammer back and pointing between Shane's eyes.

"Try me, Ryan. You think I won't? All I have to do is say you attacked me. Self-defense trumps any reason Captain Hawkins has for wanting to hollow that brain of yours out and turn you into a flesh suit for one of these spooks."

Shane raised an eyebrow and glanced at the two spirits. Hawkins wanted the Reaper ghosts to possess him. The lobotomy attempt made sense now. He thought he could use Shane's abilities if he lost his mind; to make him easier for a ghost to possess.

Ghost possession was an ugly business and rarely successful. Someone needed to be beaten down to let a ghost in. Sometimes physically, but definitely mentally. Only a strong ghost could hope to pull it off, too. But if someone's brains had been scrambled, that would make the job easier. Hell, it was actually a clever plan. Shane was impressed.

"Then do it," Shane said slowly. He took a step forward and cut the distance between them to a single stride. "Blow my brains out."

CHAPTER 20

DEAD MEN

Patton closed the gap. Shane felt the cold steel of the Sig Sauer between his eyes. The lieutenant's arm was rigid, not a shake or a twitch. He was not nervous or unsure of what to do. He wanted it so plainly that Shane could see it all over his face.

Shane knew Patton had never liked him, but he had not realized it was a matter of hatred. He didn't think they knew each other well enough for hate to have formed. He stared past the barrel of the weapon at the man himself, each with their eyes locked on the other.

There was hate there, but Shane wondered if it was for him. Patton could not have developed such animosity based on their limited time serving together. This was something different. This was something Shane had seen in other men.

It was not a common thing, but not rare enough for him to be surprised to see it now. Some soldiers, like Patton, liked the power of being soldiers. They liked being trained to kill. They liked having a gun in their hand. And when they were in the thick of things, when no reasonable person could question their motives, they liked to kill. They wanted to kill. That was what Shane saw in Patton's eyes.

People who wanted death found ways to get it. Not everyone had to murder someone for thrills and hide the body in a basement. Some found legitimate ways to act on their fantasies. Patton was one of them.

"Boss man will be very displeased with you, Alex," Shane said. The taunt did not seem to faze him.

"You think that will save you? I never agreed to this plan. You being here means it failed already, and it's not like we can just send you back. There's only one option left, the way I see it."

"Then why are you still talking?" Shane asked.

The fleshless ghost glanced at the stabbed woman and then put a hand on Patton's shoulder, causing him to wince and shrug it off.

"Mind your goddamn business," he said, momentarily taking the gun from Shane's head.

"Captain Hawkins wants him."

Patton rounded on the ghost. Though the skinless man had almost a foot in height on Patton, the smaller man still stared him down.

"Don't forget your place, Meat," Patton said.

"I'd give the same advice to you," the ghost called Meat countered.

Patton looked like he was biting back a retort and then lowered his weapon. He tucked it into his belt and stepped back.

"Fine. We keep him alive. Subdue the prisoner," he ordered.

The skinless man turned on Shane and grinned, the muscles of his cheeks pulling at his lipless mouth to expose teeth that dripped red.

"Seems bad," Hugo said.

"Seen worse," Shane whispered. "Keep an eye on the other one."

Hugo circled Shane, watching the stabbed woman who had made no attempt to get involved.

Meat lunged at Shane like they were in a wrestling match. Hands that felt like they were coated in ice grabbed at him and snagged one of his wrists. Shane countered with a punch to the ghost's exposed abdominal muscles just below the ribs.

The ghost grunted and hunched forward. No flesh on his face made the look of surprise more profound as his lidless eyes seemed to bulge and the forehead muscles rose in shock. They had not told him what Shane could do.

Shane capitalized on the ghost's surprise, pulling his other hand free and winding up for a second blow to the ghost's head.

Blood splattered and soaked Shane's face, but only for an instant. Removed from the ghost, it faded in the air, and Shane struck out again.

His knuckles hit the spirit's teeth and a pair of them crunched, falling into the already blood-filled mouth.

The ghost spit the teeth and blood into Shane's face. A thick layer of red sludge obscured his vision, and he stumbled back. Though it vanished quickly, it had the desired effect. Meat was on top of him, forcing him to the ground with a furious growl.

Shane's head hit the ground hard. His vision swam, but he focused on another shape in his peripheral vision. More ghosts had entered the room, watching from the sidelines while Shane and his bloody foe jockeyed for position, each trying to get the upper hand.

Where there had just been the two with Patton at first, Shane could now see at least a dozen shadowy forms. The longer they fought, the more appeared. Soon it was not just ghosts. Reapers had made their way to the room, the living soldiers laughing and pointing out aspects of the fight.

Shane pulled at Meat's arm as the ghost choked him. With no flesh to shield him, the muscles were exposed and easy to manipulate. He felt the ghost's brachioradialis tear free in his grasp as he yanked it from the bone and tossed it aside.

Meat howled, not in pain but in anger. He lost his ability to apply force, and his arm became weak.

Shane latched onto the ghost's chest and pried the pectoral muscles from his ribs. Meat screeched and tried to retreat but only succeeded in making Shane's work easier. Slabs of bloody muscle tore away and vanished in Shane's hands.

The Reapers were actively cheering in the background, but most of the ghosts watched in silence. Shane's hopes of escape were gone, and he knew it, but he could still save himself. Hawkins wanted him alive. He needed to make sure he stayed that way.

"Go," Patton said.

Shane looked up in time to see the ghost of the stabbed woman descending on him. He bucked the fleshless ghost off and rolled aside. She raked a hand with nails like knives down his back instead of catching his face, and he bit back a scream.

He could feel blood saturating the back of his shirt. The ghost lined up for a second strike, but Hugo caught her arm, rolling his body away from her while he held fast and snapped off the appendage.

The crowd roared. Only about a dozen men were present, and many more ghosts, but they were all in now. Shane had no time to watch how things played out with Hugo. He got to his knees quickly and plunged a hand up under the jaw of the skinned ghost, forcing his fingers into the suprahyoid muscles.

He squeezed his fingers into a fist and pulled the ghost's head down to meet him. Shane's free arm swung around in a brutal left hook, smashing the side of the ghost's head next to his eye. The hit would normally have sent the ghost reeling, but Shane held fast to the neck muscles.

As the ghost's body lurched, he moved with it, taking Meat to the ground. He was aiming to take the top of the ghost's head in his hands, but the spirit threw his head back at the last second. Instead of the top of his skull, Shane found the ghost's eyes.

His fingers pierced the cold, gelatinous orbs. Meat howled like an animal, and Shane felt the vibrations through the neck muscles. He followed through as quickly as he could, forcing his hands together.

The ghost's jaw broke as did the orbital bones around his eyes. Meat's face collapsed with a bloody crunch that sent pieces flying. For half a heartbeat, Shane was on his knees, up to his wrists inside the ghost's hollowed-out skull, and then, the body exploded.

Shane flew back against the wall, and the blast filled the room. The Reapers were knocked back, with Patton taking the worst of it. His body was dashed against the nearest table, the edge causing his back to bend the wrong way and eliciting a scream of pain from the man before he fell to the ground.

The ghosts took the blast more easily, but most still shielded themselves as the release of energy washed over them.

"One more," Hugo said suddenly.

Shane lifted his head in time to see Hugo's hand pulling the spine from the stabbed woman's back. Her body shuddered but as the bones pulled free from the skull, Hugo punched down on her head, popping it like a balloon.

The second blast knocked several ghosts back through walls, and the living Reapers face-first against them. Shane curled up and shielded his face, avoiding the brunt of the second hit but still taking enough that it slammed him against the wall a second time.

Shane unfurled his body and shakily got to his hands and knees. Across the room, two of the Reapers were already standing. One of the men had his gun drawn and aimed with a shaky arm at Shane.

"You are *so* dead, asshole," the soldier said.

"No," Hugo replied with a shake of his head. "He can't die yet."

Hugo's hunched-over and crippled body moved like something inhuman. Shane had been used to him scuttling, a half-walk like an animal. Even when he ran in the woods, he stayed in the same general position, a result of his back breaking when he was alive. It did not slow him now.

Shane's plan had been to dive behind the nearest table, flip it to block the bullets and use the knife in his pocket to take out whoever attacked him first. He didn't even make a move.

Hugo leaped like a jungle predator, arms and legs outstretched. His hands sunk into the Reaper's guts. The man fell back and when they landed, Hugo rose, his hands rising above his head and throwing the now-dead man's intestines and stomach into the air.

Blood rained down on the other Reapers. Hugo didn't pause or slow. From man to man, he moved like he was dancing. His ghostly hands entered their flesh and pulled out pieces. He removed the next man's heart and tossed it aside while his free hand took a rib bone and used it to stab the next Reaper in the temple.

Guns fired uselessly and bullets passed through Hugo's body, creating pits in the walls behind him. He raged like a rabid beast, and Shane had scarcely seen such swift and brutal carnage.

Seven corpses were at Hugo's feet before any of the men sought to escape. By then, it was already too late. He was on them in moments as they ran past the massive blast door for the exit.

Shane lost sight of the mayhem but could hear the screams. None of the spectral assets had joined the fight, though many remained in the room. Some chose to watch Hugo work, others had fled, and a handful watched Shane. Or they were waiting for Patton.

The lieutenant was still splayed out on the floor, now half-drenched in the blood of his fallen men. Shane made his way to the man's side and removed his gun as Hugo returned from the hallway. There were no sounds from the direction he had come. None of the Reapers had survived his wrath.

"Got 'em," the ghost said.

"Jesus," Shane replied. "Looks like it."

"It's okay. Don't be scared," Hugo said. "Had to do it."

"I understand," Shane said, grabbing Patton by the face and looking down at him. The lieutenant groaned, his face speckled red. His eyes fluttered, and he took a moment to focus on Shane's face.

"Someone kill him!" Patton ordered. Shane glanced up at the remaining spectral assets. None moved to follow the directive.

"Think you lost your command, Alex," Shane said.

Patton looked around to see where his men had gone and caught sight of the corpses near the blast door.

"Oh, God," he muttered. He looked back at Shane, his eyes widened, and he shook his head.

"You can't kill me. I know where Hawkins is. You can't kill me," he sputtered.

CHAPTER 21

NEXT IN LINE

"I *can* kill you, Alex. I don't want you thinking you have more value than you do." Shane said.

"No! I know everything. I can give you access to whatever you want. You can take his money, bring in the feds… you can kill him. I can help you kill him," Patton pleaded.

"Gutless," Hugo said, echoing Shane's thoughts.

Patton was grasping at any straw he could. He had turned on Hawkins so fast that it was almost shocking.

"Give me a reason to keep you alive," Shane told him.

The blood was already starting to thicken on the floor around the lieutenant. His men lay in heaps where Hugo had dropped them, and the room smelled like death. The human body was unpleasant in its final moments as various muscles relaxed. Hugo had also torn badly into some of their bodies, exposing stomachs and intestines. It got viler by the second.

"Silvershore has a new client," Patton said, stumbling over his words in his eagerness to get them out. "Hawkins has been building a new platoon, an upgraded group of Reapers with hand-picked spectral assets. The best of the best! You've never seen anything like it. Never even imagined it."

"You giving me info or an infomercial?" Shane asked.

"These are curated spectral assets, not the dregs stuck in the base here. They're trained and molded, Ryan. They're goddamn bespoke, do you understand?"

"Fancy ghosts. Got it," he replied. Patton wasting time trying to sell Shane on the idea of an elite boogeyman force was not something he had patience for. "Where is Hawkins?"

"He's gone to meet the client. This will be their first deployment. If Hawkins makes this deal, the Reapers will be installed and sanctioned, a fully operational squad with full military authority in the middle of a Central American nightmare that the U.S. government already wants distance from. We're going to own that country. It will be worth billions."

"We, huh?" Shane said. "You sure you're still part of this, Alex?"

Patton made a face and gritted his teeth.

"The point is, it's happening today. You can trash-talk me if you want or you can go stop Hawkins, but you can't do both."

Shane looked at Hugo and then at the pile of corpses by the door. There was no turning back from the road they were on now, and Shane had one chance to put an end to Hawkins. Even if he succeeded, he wasn't sure how he would find a way out of the situation without being put back in a hospital, or prison, for the rest of his life.

His best hope was to find a way to expose Hawkins for what he was doing. Even if no one believed the ghost part, Hawkins ran a mercenary squad and sold American soldiers to foreign dictators. There had to be a law about that. But he needed evidence, enough to prove beyond a doubt that Hawkins was guilty and that Shane had just been caught up in it.

"I need evidence," Shane said. "Emails, invoices, anything that shows what he's been up to."

"His office," Patton said eagerly. "It's all in there on his computer. You can find everything there. Enough to send him to prison. And I kept copies of everything. I recorded conversations! You can have it all if you let me live."

Shane got to his feet. Holding Patton's gun, he ordered the man to get up.

"Lead the way," Shane said.

Patton struggled to move, but Shane kept the gun trained on him.

"Save the show for someone else. Move," he ordered. He didn't trust Patton as far as he could throw him and had no sympathy if the man was injured. He could struggle through the bunker with a broken back, for all Shane cared.

The lieutenant led them down another long hallway. To the left was a gymnasium full of workout equipment in a large, empty area with mats on the floor. Shane assumed that the living Reapers used this for fight training. To the right was a cafeteria, with multiple tables set up and a military-style kitchen in the back. Everything was pristine as though it had never been used. A handful of ghosts milled about, silently watching Shane and Patton as they passed.

"Everyone's deployed?" Shane asked.

"Except for the men you just killed," Patton answered.

"Why were you held back?"

"Holding down the fort," Patton said. "Just in case we're needed. You tripped the alarm when you opened the blast door, and we saw you on camera. If you'd come yesterday, you would have squared off with three times as many Reapers. You'd be a smudge on a wall right now."

"Shoulda, woulda, coulda," Shane said.

They pressed onward to the end of the hall and reached a locked door with the number five on it.

"This is Hawkins' office," Patton said. "It's locked, but I can get the keys if—"

The sound of gunfire cut him off. Shane shot the lock on the door until the handle fell off and the door creaked open.

"I have keys," Shane said.

Hugo went in first, then Shane had Patton follow. Lights came on automatically, illuminating a room decorated like it belonged to a Texas oilman. There was even a football trophy on a shelf.

"Watch him," Shane told Hugo, crossing the room to the desk and the laptop that sat on top of it. Shane powered it up and looked over the top at Patton.

"Password?" he asked.

"I don't know," the man said. Shane glanced at Hugo and then back at Patton.

"I'm going to ask again, and I need you to remember that if you don't know the password, then I don't need you for anything."

"If I give you the password, you don't need me for anything," the lieutenant said.

"Hugo, what's something Alex doesn't need?"

"Left ear," Hugo said without hesitation.

Before Shane or Patton could say anything, the ghost took hold of the lieutenant's ear and pulled. Patton screamed as the flesh tore from the side of his face. He raised a hand and collapsed to his knees, blood gushing between his fingers as he held the exposed, pulpy mass where his ear had once been.

"Son of a bitch," Patton growled, half sobbing as blood and spit flowed from his face and pooled on the ground. Shane had not intended to remove the man's ear, but he had not said anything to Hugo to prevent it.

"Password?" Shane said again.

"I don't know his goddamn password!" Patton shouted.

"You said you knew what files were on his computer, Alex. Do you want me to believe you were just guessing? You, who recorded conversations and very clearly planned for a situation just like this, when you might need to double-cross Hawkins?"

Patton spit into the pool of blood, his breath coming in deep, pained shudders.

"How do I know you're not going to just kill me and leave me down here?"

"You don't," Shane said. "What is this game you think we're playing?

I'm not striking a deal with you. You give me what I need, and quickly, and maybe I'll leave without killing you. The more time you waste, the more likely that letting you live is a liability for me. Do you understand that?"

"I should have killed you when I had the chance," the other man muttered bitterly.

"I should have invested in Apple. Cry me a river. Or bleed me one."

Hugo pushed his fingers through Patton's hand and into the ruined hole that was once his ear. Patton screamed and thrashed, trying to pull the ghost's hand away but finding nothing physical to grab hold of. Shane could see Hugo's muscles moving and realized the ghost was somehow manipulating his fingers but couldn't say for sure what he was doing. It was painful, though.

"Stop," Patton screamed. "STOP!"

"Password," Hugo said calmly, not moving his hand.

In a ragged, broken voice, Patton belted out a series of numbers and letters. Shane typed them in, and the computer booted up. He nodded to Hugo, and the ghost slowly pulled his hand from Patton. The lieutenant collapsed, breathing heavily and sobbing.

Shane quickly opened folders, glossing over files for anything of interest. There was far too much information to read with the time he had at his disposal.

"Where is Hawkins having this meeting today, Alex?" Shane asked.

He opened Hawkins' email account and began attaching files, then filled out an email address and typed a quick message.

Patton sputtered on the floor and groaned. Shane typed faster, reading file names and folders, and then attaching them to emails.

"I can't hear you, Alex," he said.

"Go to hell," Patton mumbled.

"Hugo, take one of his toes," Shane suggested.

The ghost did not hesitate, but Patton cried out and rolled away to protect himself.

"New York!" he yelled out. "He's in New York City!"

"Hold on, Hugo," Shane said. "Where?"

"They're meeting in a hotel. It's the truth. I swear it's the truth."

"Hyatt Grand Central," Shane said, looking at Hawkins' schedule. "How swanky."

He finished what he was doing, closed the windows he was working in, and then closed the top of the computer.

"You've been very helpful, Alex," Shane said, looking around. The walls were paneled with auburn wood, but a visible seam ran through a panel near the rear corner of the room.

"What's that?" Shane asked, approaching it. The panel was the size of a door but there was no visible handle. Patton didn't bother to answer, and Shane pressed against the center of it. A mechanism clicked, and the door popped open.

Shane stepped into a small storage room that looked very familiar. Aluminum shelves were lined with boxes of various sizes, each one labeled with a name, date, and a brief description. It was very similar to the basement of the hospital where Shane had found Hugo.

Numerous boxes were already open, and Shane could see they were lined with lead. Others remained closed and sealed with a simple clasp.

"A. Daniels. 1991. Serial killer," Shane read on one of the box labels. "F. Tenta. 1977. Electrocution."

The room was Hawkins' armory, the place where he stored his spectral assets. Many, as Patton had said, were deployed, and the items were taken. But a good number remained behind.

"I know these two," Hugo said. He was behind Shane, looking at a different shelf.

"From the hospital?" Shane asked, reading the labels. "J. Barbieri, 1964, arson. M. Teague, 1999, axe murder."

"We should bring them," Hugo suggested.

"An arsonist and an axe murderer?" Shane asked with a raised eyebrow.

"Yes."

"I'm going to need a distraction to get inside, probably. Not carnage."

Hugo offered a half-hearted shrug.

"Talk to Barbieri. Good guy. Helpful."

Shane opened the box labeled Barbieri and looked inside. A small, black thing rested in the corner that smelled faintly of smoke. He looked around the room, but there was no sign of the ghost.

"Where is he?" Shane asked.

Hugo pointed and Shane saw a figure in the darkness behind the shelves. He was tall and thin, but mostly tucked away in shadows.

"Barbieri?" Shane asked. Hugo snorted a laugh for some reason, and the hidden ghost shuffled.

"Yeah," the ghost replied. "What do you want?"

"Hugo tells me you're a handy guy. I need help getting to someone who's going to have ghost guards. I need someone who can create a distraction. That you?"

"Who's Hugo?"

"Jester," Hugo said. Shane could still not see Barbieri clearly, but he looked bone thin.

"Oh. I don't know. I don't like being down here."

"Not here. Out there," Hugo said.

"Where?" the hidden ghost asked.

"Out in the world. Real world."

Barbieri made a humming sound.

"What do I need to do?"

"Hugo says you do fires. Maybe something to draw attention when we get where we're going. He's going to have spectral assets watching his back."

"What's that?"

"Where Zircher sent the others," Hugo answered. "What he was trying to make."

Barbieri growled, and Shane saw a flash of movement in the shadows. Burned bone, maybe. A ribcage, and an arm.

"Yeah. Yeah, I can set a fire."

"Good," Shane replied.

Shane didn't have time to play get-to-know-you with all of Hugo's dead friends, but he was satisfied that Barbieri understood what was needed. He closed the box and Barbieri disappeared.

"Did you leave Patton alone?" he asked suddenly.

"Dead," Hugo answered.

"Dead?"

Shane went back to the door and looked out into Hawkins' office. Patton was face-down on the ground where Shane had last seen him. He didn't doubt Hugo's claim, but he wanted to see for himself. There was no movement and no sign of breathing. He was dead.

"How?" Shane asked. A lost ear was painful but not life-threatening.

"Killed him," Hugo answered simply.

Shane wasn't sure what answer he was expecting, but that made all the sense in the world. Hugo was coming out of his shell since they'd escaped the hospital, but he was far more unpredictable than Shane had expected. He hoped he would not regret his decision to take the ghost.

"We should go," he said. It would be morning by the time they reached Manhattan. He didn't want to miss Hawkins.

"Them?" Hugo asked, pointing to the two boxes.

An arsonist and an axe murderer. They could probably use the backup.

Shane grabbed both, and they left.

CHAPTER 22
DEATH IN THE BIG CITY

Shane went through Patton's pockets and pulled out a set of keys. Some of the ghosts that had watched Hugo's bloodbath in the common room had followed them. They stayed on the edges of the room, lurking in corners, but watched Shane as he looted the keys from Patton.

"You can leave," Hugo told some of them as they made their way out.

"And go where?" one spirit asked.

"Nice forest outside," he said.

Shane ignored them and headed down the hall to an elevator. He and Hugo took it upstairs and found themselves in the basement of Hawkins' house.

"Should have asked how many ghosts this man had with him," Hugo said as they left the elevator through a secret door panel in a basement rec room. There was no sound in the house, and the lights in the basement were out.

"I would have, if he was alive," Shane said.

"Seemed like we were done," Hugo said. He had killed Patton so they could move on. Maybe there was more of a reason behind Hugo being in the hospital than he had let on. Regardless, Shane had hitched his wagon to the ghost, and it looked like they were seeing it through together.

He paused as the elevator door closed and returned to the hidden bunker, listening for any sign that anyone living remained in the house.

The ghosts had abandoned their posts, the commotion underground having drawn them away. Nothing remained in the house when Shane went up the stairs to the main floor.

He slipped out the front door and found Patton's vehicle parked out front, an ostentatious Escalade the man had painted matte black for some reason.

"I can still drop you off anywhere you want to go, Hugo," Shane said once the ghost was in the vehicle with him. "You've already saved my life; you definitely don't owe me anything."

"Nah," the ghost said. "Let's go."

Shane nodded and started the vehicle. The casual violence Hugo displayed fit with his personality, but the savagery was unexpected. Shane hoped he wasn't making a mistake by keeping him around. On the other hand, if Hawkins had a unit of Reapers with him, Hugo could be invaluable. He was more dangerous than even Radek Dorn and Oleg the Brute had been.

The trip to Manhattan would be just about two hours, and then they'd have to manage New York traffic. It would be early when they arrived, and Shane feared that rush hour would already be underway. The last thing he wanted was to spend an hour stuck in New York gridlock when Hawkins was just a stone's throw away.

Hawkins was booked at the Hyatt Grand Central. Times Square was the only more noticeable place in the city for them to go. It was a strange place to do business, but it fit with what Shane knew about Hawkins since he'd left the Marines. He was a venal man. Why wouldn't he stay in a big, obnoxious hotel in the heart of the city?

The crowds might work in Shane's favor, keeping the Reapers from overstepping themselves. On the other hand, the spectral assets would not be bound by any such restrictions. Maybe that was why Hawkins chose the place. If he had a client lined up, he might be using the location to show off how they could work in plain sight.

Hugo stared out the windows in awe as they made their way through upstate New York. The sun had risen, and the traffic was bad but not as awful as Shane expected. It was still early though, and they had a ways to go before they reached Grand Central.

"So many people," the ghost said, watching everything they passed with great interest.

"Too many," Shane agreed. He hated Boston because of the crowds. New York City, and Manhattan especially, was his idea of a nightmare.

The streets filled as they got closer to their goal. They took the Midtown tunnel into the city, and Hugo marveled at all the cars. Shane watched ghosts wander the sides of the road, unseen by most drivers, loitering like people waiting for buses that never came.

The Escalade emerged into Manhattan, and traffic slowed. They'd have to pass through one of the densest, busiest parts of the city. He couldn't imagine getting to Hawkins without making a scene.

"So many people," Hugo said again. Shane ignored him this time. He could see their destination ahead, a massive tower of glass with flags mounted out front waving in the breeze.

"This is it up here," Shane said. "Keep your eyes open for anything suspicious."

He drove past the entrance of the hotel and saw what he was looking for. Six men stood on the sidewalk out front, each a short distance from the other and looking inconspicuous. One pretended to read a magazine, another was on his phone, and a third drank coffee. Each man had a ghost within arm's length. They were clearly guarding the entrance, either because Hawkins expected trouble or because he wanted to put on a show for his prospective clients. Either way, it meant the same thing for Shane. Getting access to the hotel would be a challenge.

"There are more," Hugo said as they passed the hotel. He pointed up, and Shane saw upper windows reflecting the city back at them, but a pair of ghosts lingered outside, suspended above the street and getting a bird's eye view of what lay below.

"I clocked eight," Shane said. "Have to be more inside."

It couldn't be a whole platoon; that would be too many men. A squad or two was not out of the question, though. Hawkins was brokering a big deal. There could have been dozens of Reapers in and around the area. And all he had was one unpredictable and potentially psychotic ghost with a broken back.

But that wasn't true. He had two boxes.

Shane circled the block and came back out front of the hotel, looking for a place to park. He might as well have been looking for a unicorn.

Deftly, he pulled over across from the hotel and stopped in the bus lane in front of a juice bar.

"Out. Quick," he told Hugo, hopping out through the passenger-side door and taking the two lead-lined boxes with him.

He relied on New Yorkers' tendency to not care what a stranger was doing when he slipped away, leaving the car parked illegally as he ducked under some scaffolding with Hugo to stay out of sight of the Reapers.

The sidewalks bustled with pedestrians and cars flooded the streets. He could see a bus coming that would soon butt up against the abandoned Escalade and cause further traffic issues. If all went well, it would create enough of a jam to provide a temporary distraction and make getting into the hotel easier.

"How trustworthy is your other friend?" Shane asked Hugo, holding up the two small boxes. The ghost shrugged in a manner that didn't instill much faith in Shane.

"Teague's quiet. Jackie's angry," Hugo replied. Neither one of those statements related to Shane's question. The bus was getting closer. If Shane wanted to capitalize on the distraction, they only had minutes.

"Who the hell is Jackie?" Shane said, looking at the boxes.

"Jackie Lantern. Barbieri. Same," Hugo assured him.

"Okay. Jackie knows what's up, is Teague going to be on board?"

"Maybe," Hugo said.

It was a terrible answer. But two ghosts that Hugo knew had to be better than ones he didn't know, Shane figured. He went for Teague first.

The clasp was stiff, and Shane had to work it to get it open. Dozens of people passed him without looking in his direction as he pulled the box open. Inside was a single gold tooth.

Teague was a man of about Shane's height. He slouched and needed a shave, and there was a bullet hole through the side of his head that had blasted a fist-sized hole of an exit wound on the other side. He blinked blood-red eyes and took a moment to focus on Shane and Hugo when he appeared.

"Jester, that you?" the ghost asked.

"Call me Hugo," he corrected. "Long time."

Teague looked around, watching people and cars go by. He reached out and touched a man in a suit talking on a Bluetooth headset. The man shuddered and looked back, but seeing nothing, kept on his way.

"Where the hell are we?"

Teague's accent sounded Midwestern. His hair was matted with blood, and his clothes, a simple button-down shirt, and khaki pants, were equally soaked. He was a bloodbath from head to toe. Shane wasn't surprised that Hugo liked him.

"New York," Hugo answered. "On a mission."

Teague looked back at Hugo, one eyebrow raised dramatically high.

"Mission?"

"This is my friend," Hugo said, gesturing to Shane. "Killed the new doctor. Killed Scarface. Now we gotta kill someone for him."

"Scarface? Who the hell is Scarface?" Teague asked.

"Dudley. Are you in?" Hugo asked.

The ghost still seemed confused, but he smiled grimly.

"Of course. Who are we killing?"

"*Who are we killing?*" Hugo repeated, looking at Shane.

"You're not killing anybody. I just need help getting to the guy. Across the street at the Hyatt, there are armed men with ghost partners. I need you to keep those guys busy long enough for me to get into the hotel."

"Keep them busy," Teague said, enunciating the words as he mulled them over.

"So, kill them," Hugo added.

"NO KILLING. I just need them distracted. If we cause a scene, then everyone panics, and I get exposed. That's not what I want," Shane clarified.

"I'm very discreet," Teague said. His tone was meant to be reassuring, but the words sounded ominous given his state. Shane didn't have time to argue and had to hope he'd at least stick to his word.

"We should get Jackie, too," Hugo said.

Shane glanced at the hotel again. How many men were inside? There had to be at least as many as those outside. A well-placed fire on the far side of the doors would draw them away.

The bus was a block away from their abandoned vehicle. It was a now-or-never situation. He had to trust Hugo.

Shane knelt and put both lead-lined boxes on the ground behind a small, potted tree outside the juice bar's door. He opened the second box. Inside was Barbieri's black, half-melted thing which, even in full light, was impossible to recognize. It was burned so badly that now it was just a golf-ball-sized mound covered in char.

The thick smell of smoke and burned meat quickly filled the air as Shane got back to his feet. Others on the street noticed it as well, looking around as though searching for the source of the fire while Shane stepped away from the boxes.

Flames licked at the scaffolding, causing Shane to step back and shield his eyes. No one else on the street saw a thing as fire twisted up and raged around the skeletal form of a man.

The figure immersed in fire still had some flesh on its body, but not much. Fire had consumed it almost completely. The bones were charred as black as the ghost's haunted item, and its face was barely more than a fire-filled skull with bits of bubbling flesh and fat smeared across it.

The flaming skeleton opened its black jaws and screamed. The sound echoed under the scaffolding and filled 42nd Street, rising above the drone of engines and horns.

Pedestrians visibly recoiled, especially those closest to the spirit. They saw nothing but heard the blood-curdling wail like the sound of an animal in a slaughterhouse.

Those in the immediate area either ran in fear or froze, trying to source the terrible sound. Cars stopped and people on the far side of the street stopped to stare in confused fear or concern. There was no way the Reapers had not heard it.

"Jackie," Hugo said, smiling at the burning horror.

Flame-filled eye sockets turned to face Hugo, and a burning, skeletal hand rose. The ghost waved.

This was not what Shane had seen in Hawkins' office. Or, rather, it was, but it was hidden behind shelves. There had been no fire then, no burning stench, and certainly no nightmarish cries. Jackie Lantern was not here to play around.

"We need to do this now," Shane said. The bus was stuck behind the Escalade, and a police cruiser had stopped alongside it. Time was up.

CHAPTER 23

BURNING THROUGH

"I need to get into that hotel without the Reapers and their ghosts out front seeing me," Shane said. "Go to the far side. If you can get there and there are no people nearby, you can set a small fire and draw the Reapers' attention while Hugo and I sneak inside. Teague, you can come in behind and keep them busy between you and Jackie until I'm out of sight."

The flaming ghost's hollow skull burned like it was filled with gasoline. Shane could feel no heat off of it, but the street smelled like a barbecue that had long since gotten out of control. Char and burned meat filled the air. The fact that Shane knew what kind of meat he was smelling made it worse. At least the commuters would have thought it was pork.

"He's going after the man who took you from the hospital," Hugo said. "He's in the hotel."

Hugo pointed across the street. Jackie Lantern turned his head, and his flames rose higher.

The ghost shrieked again, and this time, people on the street cried out in surprise and fear and then ran without knowing why. Shane felt a blast of cold from the raging orange flames, the contrast playing havoc on his senses.

Without another sound, the ghost left. He ran into the street, trailing fire like a living cloak of orange-yellow fury. Black smoke rose in thick, impossible-to-miss plumes into the sky like a raging oil fire in motion.

"What the hell is he doing?" Shane cried out.

Jackie put his hands on the hood of an idling Yellow Cab. The car burst into flames, and now, dozens of people on the street were screaming.

The ghost did not pause but ran to the next car, swiping a hand over the hood and causing it to fly back as the engine exploded.

"Distraction," Hugo said. "He improvises."

The Reapers had congregated near the eastern side of the hotel to watch as Jackie Lantern stormed toward them. The flaming ghost ran up the hood of another car, setting it ablaze with his feet, and then stood in the tower of black smoke that rose around him.

Jackie threw back his head and howled, belching fire into the sky. It rose like a geyser and filled the air. Drivers fled their cars as fire and smoke danced from one to the next, seemingly with a life of its own. No one could see Jackie's hands directing the fire to and fro like he was conducting an orchestra of destruction.

The nightmarish sound that came from the ghost's skeletal mouth, along with the flaming mayhem left in his wake, caused an immediate panic. Dozens of people ran in every direction as cars were abandoned and traffic ground to a halt.

"Jesus," Shane muttered. This had not been the plan at all.

"God, I missed that guy," Teague said. His bloody smile was wide and cheerful as he glanced at Shane and Hugo. "What are you waiting for?"

Teague ran into the fray, passing through flaming cars at a run to the far side of the street. Shane followed suit, dodging wide of the burning wrecks as he cut across the street, through the traffic jam and panicked pedestrians.

Screams came from all corners. Some people chose to duck for cover behind parked cars; others ran into the nearest open businesses or down the street to the next block. The lone police officer who was investigating the abandoned Escalade was trying to maintain order. He was out of his depth.

Jackie Lantern reached a FedEx delivery truck stopped in front of the Hyatt entrance. Reapers were shouting orders to one another as their spectral assets circled the flaming ghost. None reached him in time.

The ghost plunged a hand into the truck's gas tank. Shane was already diving for cover as he saw it happen. The truck exploded and debris flew in all directions.

The massive ball of fire rose high into the air. Chunks of metal and flaming packages rained in all directions.

Reapers closed in on Jackie, but none took notice of Teague until he was already upon them. The one-time axe murderer set upon the first of Hawkins' men and snapped his neck in the middle of the sidewalk in the glow of the flaming delivery truck.

Sirens wailed in the near distance. New York City police had appeared several blocks down, impeded by the traffic jam Jackie had created. Officers on foot would arrive soon.

Shane had wanted a distraction, but he had been given a war zone. There was no way Hawkins was unaware of what was happening. If he had not tried to get ahold of Dr. Loomis, he would do so now, and when he discovered the man was dead, his next call would be to the FBI. Shane needed to tighten the noose and fast.

Another vehicle exploded, and Jackie shrieked like a banshee, the sound sending a shiver down Shane's spine. Shane kept low to the ground, running like any other panicked pedestrian, only his goal was the hotel doors.

Other bystanders had made for the Hyatt as well, trying to hide anywhere that would offer cover. Shane did what he could to blend in. He kept his eyes down and ran, pushing through the nearest door and ignoring the Reapers. He made it into the lobby just as another vehicle went up in flames.

Jackie was intent on setting fire to the entire street. To the average New Yorker, it must have looked like the most baffling chain of events with no explanation. Fire leaped with a mind of its own from car to car. Only Shane and the Reapers could see what was really happening, and the Reapers were ill-equipped to handle the problem. They were partnered with the dead, but they had no power over them.

From the hotel lobby, Shane looked back in time to see Teague break another Reaper's neck. The man fell in front of the doors, his gun drawn. Someone inside screamed, and Shane heard the word "terrorist".

There were armed men and exploding cars on the street. The final fuse had been lit.

The Hyatt lobby was now full of panicked civilians, most of them hiding behind the check-in desk and the lobby furnishings. Dozens of people were on the phone with the police or loved ones. A handful were even live streaming what was happening on social media. It was absolute chaos.

Hugo appeared shortly after Shane entered, slinking along out of sight as Shane skirted behind the check-in desk. He needed to find Hawkins' room as quickly as he could.

A gunshot outside caused a new round of screams. It was followed by an answering shot, and then several more. The Reapers were shooting at the police, but it was unclear who had started the firefight.

Jackie Lantern howled, the sound causing more screams of fear in the lobby, and another car exploded. East 42nd Street had turned into a battlefield.

Shane got to his feet, weaving through a dozen frightened people, and accessed the nearest computer. The last employee had not logged out. He searched for Hawkins' name and found his room number.

The glass doors of the Hyatt exploded inward as a flaming man burst through them, screaming, and flailing his arms. The lobby filled with hysterical cries. The burning man made it all of five feet before falling to the floor and writhing in agony as the fire consumed the last bit of life left in him.

A ghost watched the man die, and Shane realized it had been a Reaper. His spectral asset was a spirit with an average build, sunken eyes, and pale, waxy flesh. The ghost stared across the lobby and locked eyes with Shane as smoke from his partner rose in thick, acrid clouds.

"Here!" the ghost yelled. "He's here!"

Shane cursed and looked around. There were too many people in the lobby to fight anyone, living or dead. If someone streamed a video of him fighting a ghost in the flaming ruins of a New York hotel, he could kiss any hope of clearing his name and going back to a normal life goodbye.

Two of the Reapers came to the door along with their ghosts. Teague fought with another spectral asset on the street behind them as Jackie set fire to the bus behind the Escalade.

Gunshots rang out from both sides of the street. Much of the screaming had died down, as those who could flee had mostly all done so.

One of the Reapers in the doorway raised a gun and began firing. Shane ducked, and those around him screamed, many covering their ears and curling into a ball as chunks of the wall exploded and showered down.

The Reaper reached the desk and Shane stood quickly, took the computer keyboard and swung it as hard as he could, smashing the Reaper in the face.

The man fell, blood spewing from his mouth, and a few civilians cheered. A second round of gunshots silenced everyone as the next Reaper took aim, grazing Shane's shoulder and causing him to drop to the floor.

"What the hell are you doing?" a hotel employee hissed, tears in her eyes as she held her hands over her head.

"Just trying to stay alive," Shane replied.

The second Reaper appeared at the edge of the desk, and Shane's fist was already in motion before the other man could aim his weapon. He struck the man in the groin as hard as he could, causing him to drop to his knees.

Hugo was on the Reaper the moment he dropped. To everyone else in the lobby, the injured man simply went rigid and slammed his own face hard into the edge of the desk before falling back unconscious with a broken nose.

"Stay down. Police will be here soon," Shane told the woman and the others hidden behind the desk. He ducked around the corner past the fallen Reaper and headed down the hall.

The spectral assets pursued him, swiftly and silently, drifting unseen through the hotel lobby. Shane needed a place to duck out of sight where he could fight without causing an even bigger scene.

Out on the street, the bus' gas tank finally went up. The explosion was the biggest yet, shaking the Hyatt as though a bomb had gone off and shattering the lobby windows.

Shane used the noise to mask the sound of the stairwell door as he opened it and slipped inside. The stairwell was empty, and the noise inside was muffled by the walls. The screams were dull and faded, and the gunshots on the street were almost impossible to hear.

It took only a moment for the first of the spectral assets to show up, the one who had outed Shane to begin with. The moment the waxy face appeared through the wall and into the stairwell, Shane's fist collided with the dead man's jaw, knocking him to his hands and knees in front of the stairs.

The ghost snapped back quickly, and tried to get to his feet. Shane hit him again and then knelt, forcing the ghost back to the floor. He held the ghost's head in his hands and began to squeeze.

"Let him go," a voice said from the door. A second spirit had arrived, this one a tall, lanky man with sores all over his face as though he'd suffered a serious infection before death.

"If you like," Shane replied. He squeezed harder and crushed the first spirit's head.

The blast rocked the stairwell and knocked Shane and the ghost backward. The spirit fell onto Hugo, who quickly removed the other ghost's head, leading to a second explosion.

Muffled screams sounded from somewhere out in the lobby, and Shane realized that the spirits' haunted items must have exploded on the bodies of the Reapers who carried them. There were still more on the way, and they had no time to waste.

"Let's go," Shane said to Hugo, taking the stairs two at a time. "Before your buddy Jackie burns down the hotel."

CHAPTER 24
TRAPPED

Hawkins' room was on the thirtieth floor of the Hyatt. Shane couldn't risk taking the elevator that far with so many Reapers around. He knew they wouldn't be above cutting the wires and sending him plummeting to his death in the hotel basement.

He took the stairs as quickly as he could, glancing over the railing on every floor to see where the Reapers from outside were. He could see only one following, about six floors below him, but there was no sign of the spirit that must be in tow.

Hotel guests stopped him on more than one floor to ask what was happening and if it was safe to go down. In each case, he told them it was probably best to return to their rooms and lock the door.

Hugo kept pace up the stairs, running on all fours at his side. They were outpacing the Reaper giving chase, but not by much. By the time Shane got to the right floor, he'd have just a short time to prepare for the Reaper's arrival.

The farther up they traveled, the less noise Shane could hear from the street, but it had not gone completely silent. There were still explosions, and the appearance of a swift, staccato rumbling alerted him to the presence of a police helicopter. Things had gone to hell outside. His only real satisfaction now was that he knew there was no way Hawkins had wanted the Reapers to engage with cops, and they had made a serious blunder.

Shane was winded by the time he hit the twenty-ninth floor and began to ascend the final flight. He slowed his pace when he saw what awaited him. It was not the stairwell as it had been all the way up. Within two steps, he found himself in a fractured version of the stairs, dimly lit and hazy with dust caked on the steps and cracked tile lining the walls.

Light fixtures were broken, the edges of the lights dangling old cobwebs that drifted softly in barely felt air currents.

He turned, looking back the way he'd come, and the old stairs were gone. The hotel was a relic to his eyes, a forgotten and abandoned old thing. Hugo was gone, and the muffled sounds of Jackie and Teague's war had vanished. Shane was in the ghostly ruins of some spirit's illusion, a fantasy meant to trap him. Hawkins had set a spirit as a guard, and it must have been a powerful one.

Shane slowed his pace, watching where he was going as he continued to make his way to the thirtieth-floor exit. Broken tile crumbled underfoot, and he could smell the old, earthy smell of the dust as his boots kicked up clouds of it with each new step.

He could see nothing move, and there were no places for things to hide on the way up. He was not walking into an ambush, at least not immediately. The ghost who had crafted the illusion, however, had been incredibly thorough and detailed. Everything looked, felt, and smelled real.

With no choice but to play the game, Shane continued up the last couple of steps and reached the door marked thirty. Where the Hyatt had once been pristine and clean, the door was stained with mildew and caked-on filth around the handle.

Shane pulled at the door handle and rusted hinges squeaked painfully as though the door had not been opened in many years. The smell that came from the hallway was hot and thick. It reminded him of a swamp, some densely forested part of the bayou where the sun could never get through the trees and the water could sit warm and stagnant for months on end.

The hallway carpet squished underfoot as Shane left the stairwell. Tiny, flying insects buzzed in clouds and huddled together in masses around puddles of still water on the floor. The stink of decaying matter was as strong as he had ever smelled it.

The humidity clung to his face and, after his run up the stairs, Shane could already feel sweat trickling down the small of his back. It settled above his eyes and lips, thick and damp and distracting.

A dead body lay on the floor a few feet from the door. The flesh had long ago been stripped away, and the filth-covered bones were now home to fungus and moss growth. The bottom jaw was missing, and insect larvae slithered about in the darkness of the skull.

Shane stepped past it warily, expecting it to rise and attack, but it did not. The rotten hallways stretched onward, beckoning him to follow the filth-laden path to his destination.

The heat increased as he walked. His shirt was becoming saturated. He had expected freezing cold temperatures, something typical of the dead. The swampy illusion was an unwelcome surprise.

Shane walked slowly and carefully. He avoided the larger puddles and shooed away swarms of gnats and mosquitos. He knew they were not real; they were things constructed of the same ephemera that gave a ghost form. But his abilities to fight ghosts, to interact with them physically, made the illusions more real than simple ghostly visions. They could kill if he wasn't careful.

As he walked, he began to pick up a faint sound somewhere ahead. When he stopped to listen, straining to hear the very quiet sound, the insects of the ghostly swamp settled on his flesh, sticking to the sweat, and making him itch.

He walked slowly and silently, listening to what sounded like a strangled, desperate wheezing. The sound grew louder as he approached an open door, the first one he saw along the hallway.

The dim light filled the room, filtered through layers of sludge that was caked on the windows. There was a bed, but it was overgrown with moss and mold. Tangled, snake-like vines encircled much of it, and tepid water covered the floor, making a home to hundreds of insects that danced across the surface.

The ghost sat atop the bed, half splayed out and half slumped over as though it had been sitting up. The ghost's flesh was as rotten as the rest of the swamp, blistered with ugly brown and yellow pustules that were swollen and glossy. It breathed in long, raspy breaths as though trying to draw air from deep in its stomach with each labored attempt. It made a rattling and popping sound inside of its chest before it rested for a moment and then struggled to take another breath.

Shane watched the ghost's eyes flicker open. The whites were jaundiced, and the rest seemed to be all black. It stared at Shane, and he watched as a leech, fat with rancid blood, squirmed from out of one pestilence-ridden nostril on the ghost's rotten face and fell onto the bed.

"They told me you'd come," the ghost wheezed. The voice was raspy and low, barely audible from across the room. It smiled at him, and thick gobs of congealed blood teased at the edges of its lips, jiggling just so before slipping out in thick, sticky tendrils.

"I'm sure they did," Shane replied. "Where's Hawkins?"

"You should worry… about… yourself," the spirit wheezed.

It flopped over on the sludge-covered bed and then pulled itself to the edge with glistening, leathery hands. The yellow-and-black eyes stayed trained on Shane while the disgusting grin continued to leak vile ooze.

The ghost struggled, and then finally fell from the bed's edge to the wet floor. Instead of landing, however, it plunged beneath the stagnant surface and vanished.

Shane stepped back from the door, his eyes searching the pool for signs of movement. The initial ripple of the ghost's body dissipated, and only the insects remained, skittering about.

The floor went silent, save for the occasional croak of an unseen frog and the buzz of mosquito wings when they got too close to Shane's ear. The illusion was all-encompassing, unlike anything he'd experienced.

Every footfall produced a new burst of unpleasant smell. Every surface seemed alive with something dark and foreboding.

Shane left the room behind and continued down the hall. The water grew deeper the farther he went. What was once just puddles in the hotel hallway became standing water, and soon enough, it was up to his ankles. Mud and muck grew darker until the carpet was obscured. If he went any farther, he wouldn't be able to see what waited below.

Something splashed ahead of him, just near another open door. He saw a hint of something pale and fleshy vanish beneath the surface, but it had gone too fast to gauge its size.

Shane backed up, looking to return to drier land. The water continued to rise even as he retraced his steps. Soon, it was up to his shins, and back in the room where he had first seen the ghost. There was no carpet anymore and no floor. The water level rose slowly and steadily, warm and sludgy around his legs.

He cursed and trudged back to the stairwell. At least out there, he could still go up, retreat to the next floor, and plan another way to get to Hawkins. But the ghost was not allowing that.

Shane pushed open the door marked "stairs" and cursed again. The dusty, dim stairwell had vanished. There were no steps or even walls any longer. An open swamp stretched out before him, with dead, black trees bent over and dotting the landscape, and scattered clumps of weed-covered land offering barely enough room on which to stand.

The ceiling was gone, and the trees reached crooked branches up toward a pink and gray sky that showed no sign of a sun. The stale air didn't move, and the insect clouds were thicker than ever.

Gnats came for Shane's eyes and ears. He could feel their tiny feet as they climbed into his nose and chewed at the corners of his mouth. He spat and swatted at them while the high-pitched whine of mosquitos attacked him from all angles.

Shane looked back and found the hallway gone. He stood in a

freestanding doorway, with no walls, no floors, and no ceiling. The Hyatt was gone, and he was in a decaying, forgotten old swamp. Just him and the insects, nothing more in any direction.

The teeming swarms of insects swirled around him. He could hear them crawling in his ear canals and feel them going deeper into his nose even as he forcefully blew them out. Others went for the corners of his eyes, and some slipped under his eyelids, their tiny bodies like squirming pebbles as they struggled against the surface of his eyes.

More came for him and he swore again, inadvertently inviting them into his mouth. They crawled across and under his tongue, writhing against the roof of his mouth as he spit. There was only one place to go, one avenue for escape.

Shane dove headlong into the swamp, dropping into the murky, putrid water, and dunking his head beneath the surface. He swam forward, all but blind in the gloom, heading toward where he remembered the nearest chunk of semi-dry land to be.

His hands struggled in the darkness, feeling around for anything, until he finally came upon the trunk of one of the decrepit, withered trees. The surface was slimy and hard to grasp, but he kicked his feet and pushed himself toward it, using the trunk as a guide to lead him upward.

The dark water did not part for him as he rose, and he continued to kick his feet, one hand on the tree and the other reaching up for anything. There was no surface, no air, and nothing waiting for him.

Shane swam up and up but could not find the surface. The pressure in his lungs began to build, and he pumped his legs harder, pushing down with his hands. Still, he found no break.

Finally, the haze began to fade, and a faint shimmer appeared before him, still several yards above. He pushed harder, swimming with all his might until he was within inches of being free.

Something grabbed his ankle. Cold and firm, it clamped tightly just above his boot. He looked down but could see nothing. When he kicked down with his free foot, something took that ankle as well.

In a rush of movement, Shane was yanked down. His body jerked, and he plummeted as though a rock had been tied to him. He couldn't even scream, for he had no air left in his lungs.

CHAPTER 25
RELEASE

Warm, muddy water filled Shane's mouth. He felt it sliding down his throat and burning its way into his lungs. The darkness of the water closed in around him as the unseen hands dragged him down farther and farther until he felt himself being flipped.

The world spun, and suddenly he was not being pulled down, he was suspended. The water was gone, and he coughed. His hands dangled and scraped against a cold, stone floor before he was dropped in a heap.

His body told him to expel the water, but as he heaved and choked, he realized there was nothing there. He dry-heaved and nearly vomited, but there was no water. He wasn't even wet.

Shane sat up and looked around. He was in a dark, moist cavern with smooth stone floors. There was a dim light by which he could barely see, but it was sourceless, seemingly coming from all corners at once. It offered barely enough illumination to give a sense of space and nothing more.

Shane realized the ghost was wasting time. It was keeping him busy, which would allow Hawkins to escape or finish whatever business he had started. Shane needed to break the illusion and end the ghost before it trapped him in this new fantasy.

Something moved in the darkness, but Shane could not see it. He heard a dry, scraping sound a few yards away like fabric being lightly pulled across the stone. At first, he thought someone was dragging something, but as the sound continued, he realized that was not it.

He was still on his hands and knees when a form appeared. The soft shushing sound preceded it as it lurched up over the uneven stone.

It was glossy and black, a smooth, rounded body that bulged and pulsed as it came into view. The soft, scraping sound was the body surging forward, growing long and thin as it extended itself, and the back-scraping sound was the rear end of the creature pulling itself up to the head to catch up with the rest.

It was a leech, Shane realized, as it throbbed and pulsed its way toward him. A shimmering, onyx black body the size of a man. It wriggled its way toward Shane in the dark.

As it came closer, the front of the slimy creature rose up. The light gleamed off of a mouth like a ring, a head-sized circle of teeth surrounding more teeth, thousands of them in concentric rings. They quivered as the mouth pulsated and sucked at the air.

A visceral disgust twisted Shane's gut. The fight-or-flight instinct was there, and it was strong, urging him to run. It was primal and instinctual. No one should face such a monstrosity. But the urge to fight was stronger.

"I'm just about done here," Shane said.

The rows of teeth in the leech's mouth flexed and spread apart as it expanded its jaws. Shane got to his feet and pushed off the ground, lunging at the creature before it could lower itself.

The flesh of the leech felt like thickened Jell-O in his hands. It was hard to grasp, but he sunk his fingers into the meat of it until his hands were closed almost completely into fists. He dragged the thing to the ground and simultaneously drove his hands together.

A squeal erupted from the leech's mouth. The light flared around them and brightened dramatically. Cold, featureless stone was replaced by carpet, a sofa, and a mahogany desk. The cavern vanished, replaced by a hotel suite.

The leech was gone, and Shane was crouched over the rotted, leathery ghost he had seen on the bed before.

"No!" it screamed as Shane pushed his hands closer together. His fingers had sunk below the layers of stained and bloated flesh, right against the spirit's skull.

The bones snapped, and the sofa broke Shane's fall as he was tossed backward. The windows blew out, and the sound of glass shattering was barely audible over the thunder of a helicopter outside and the wail of multiple sirens.

The stench of swamp vanished, replaced by the smell of burning rubber. The streets of New York were still a war zone, and Shane was alone in an empty suite.

A gust of cold air preceded Hugo as he came through the door, looking around like an attack dog summoned by his master.

"Oh. There you are," the ghost said.

Shane exhaled loudly and sat up. He could still taste the water.

"What the hell is going on outside?" he asked.

"Jackie set some fires. He's inside now. Teague is gone."

"Great," Shane replied. "We need to find Hawkins if he's still in the building."

"Elevators don't work. No one gets out. He's here."

"What happened to the elevators?"

"Cut the cables," Hugo answered. "Killed a Reaper inside. Messy."

"Messy," Shane said, getting to his feet. "Okay."

Shane made his way to the door of the suite and opened it, peering into the hall. A bullet barely missed his head, splintering the door frame before he ducked back inside.

"You want to take that one?" Shane asked, looking back at Hugo.

"No need," Hugo said.

The scream that tore through the hallway was more than enough indication of what he meant. In an enclosed space, it was much more deafening than it had been out on the streets.

Smoke rolled along the ceiling, preceding Jackie Lantern. The flaming ghost appeared from the opposite direction, shambling down the hall toward the Reaper and trailing flaming bits that burned through the carpet and scorched the walls with each step.

The Reaper fired several rounds that passed harmlessly through Jackie's body. Without their spectral assets, the Reapers were all but useless against ghosts.

Jackie's smoldering body stumbled by Shane's open door. The skull face did not turn to look at him or Hugo; it was fixed on the Reaper. The ghost had lost the plot from the beginning, and Shane no longer cared to keep him on track. His job was to distract on the street, not hunt through the hotel, but at least he'd be clearing roadblocks.

"He seems awfully angry," Shane said as he watched the ghost pass. The Reaper fled, firing several rounds haphazardly behind him.

"He is," Hugo agreed. "Wants revenge."

"On Hawkins? How the hell does he know Hawkins?"

"Doesn't," Hugo said. "We should go."

He ducked out of the suite and followed Jackie down the hall. The trail of smoke and char went around a corner, but Shane lingered behind. The Reaper had been guarding a room, not just loitering in the hall.

Shane approached the door. It was the room that Hawkins was staying in, according to the computer Shane had accessed in the lobby. Despite everything that was going on, Hawkins had not left.

He tried the door handle, and it opened without resistance. The man hadn't even bothered to lock it. Shane let himself in, moving carefully as his eyes searched the large room ahead of him.

"I should have known," Hawkins said, surprising him. He was on the far side of the room by the minibar, looking at Shane in the mirrored backsplash.

"Should have done a lot of things," Shane replied.

Hawkins chuckled and dropped some ice cubes into a rocks glass. He poured whiskey over the two cubes and clinked them noisily, swishing the mixture around.

"Dr. Loomis wanted to just kill you outright. I said, 'No, let's just cut his brain apart,' and look where we are now. Always trust a doctor, I guess."

"I guess," Shane agreed. He looked around the room again. There was no sign of anyone else. "Thought you were up here selling yourself to some upstart equatorial dictator."

"Oh, the clients. Yes, that ship has sailed. Turns out it's hard to make a client transfer funds while someone is blowing up buses on the street below you," Hawkins said.

Shane shrugged.

"Wish I could take credit, but that wasn't me. I was aiming for something more discreet."

Hawkins downed the whiskey in a single gulp and clinked the glass back on the bar top with a nod. He refilled the glass and pointed at Shane.

"You should be dead by now. You're insufferable, you know that? Smug. Asinine. You could be a millionaire; but look at you. Mutilated, freakish, and alone. They told me you've got a whole tragic little family of ghosts in your house. A goddamn German from the war, a grim little girl, and a fat boy. Is it like your own Addams family? Do you play house in your downtime?"

He laughed heartily and finished his second drink.

"Of all the places you could die, the Hyatt isn't the worst," Shane told him.

Hawkins rolled his eyes.

"Goodness, is that where we are already? You making threats you can't follow up on? I thought we had more time."

Shane took a step toward him, and Hawkins dropped his glass, picking up a box from the bar. He recognized it immediately. There were two nearly identical boxes on the sidewalk in front of a juice bar. It had come from the basement of Dr. Loomis' hospital. Hawkins had brought another ghost.

"The look on your face tells me you know what this is. Had a trip into

Dr. Loomis' house of horrors, did you?" Hawkins asked.

"I picked up a couple of friends in yours," Shane replied.

"Is that a fact? I have to assume you've already met that swampy creep Cathcart, but I needed someone with a little more oomph for my personal protection. The kind of guy who can deal with someone like you, Ryan. An expert."

"Do I need to call room service and order lunch to get through this?" Shane asked.

Hawkins' laugh was less mirthful than his previous ones. He flipped the box over in one hand and dumped the contents into the other. Shane could not see what it was before Hawkins tucked it into his pocket.

"Goodbye, Ryan. I have no doubt we'll tell stories about you over drinks one day. Fanciful memories of what a waste you were."

Shane waited, expecting a furious monstrosity to rush him, but nothing appeared. Seconds ticked by, and finally, after nearly a minute, Hawkins smiled, and a man stepped into the room from the shadows of a nearby doorway.

Whoever the ghost was, Shane did not recognize him. He was an elderly man, with hair like snow and ears that were pushed out too far by the thick rims of his glasses.

He carried himself with a vague arrogance, his back straight, and his head up. He wore a suit that was well-tailored but also old like it had been purchased in the sixties. His shoes were finely polished but scuffed slightly at the toes, and he wore one piece of jewelry, what looked like an old class ring.

"Who are you supposed to be?" Shane asked.

"Dr. Andrew Zircher," the ghost answered. "A pleasure to meet you. Shall we begin?"

Shane recognized the last name from Hugo. He had been the doctor running the show before Dr. Loomis. He had tortured and killed Hugo and Scarface and the woman with the wired jaw. Probably every other ghost in the basement as well, part of his curation efforts. Now, he was a ghost.

"I want you to show him everything, Zircher. Make him regret ever trying to take me on."

Hawkins held a briefcase in his hand and prepared to leave the room. Shane kept an eye on the ghost of the doctor but focused on his former captain.

"You won't be leaving," Shane assured him.

"Oh, I think I will," Hawkins replied. "Haven't you heard all those sirens? I called the FBI the moment I knew you were here, Ryan. Your fires and distractions mean nothing. I know you might get past Zircher, but good luck getting past an army of armed federal agents."

"That's funny," Shane said. "I called the FBI, too. Or sent them a message anyway, with all the files from your computer. Hey, which one of us do you think they're more interested in?"

The color drained from Hawkins' face. Shane could see the muscles of the man's jaws clench and tense.

"Kill him. Make it hurt," he said.

CHAPTER 26

MAKE IT HURT

"Let us begin."

Zircher's voice echoed in the room as though the 'space was an auditorium. He held his arms outstretched dramatically as blinding, white lights flared to life on the ceiling.

Shane winced and raised a hand to protect his eyes. Then the light dimmed, and Shane saw that he was no longer in the room. He growled, anger simmering in his chest as he realized Zircher had made an illusion for him, and Hawkins was likely getting away.

"Enough of this," Shane said, storming forward. Hawkins had a thing for ghosts that played with their victims' minds. He'd had more than enough of it.

But Zircher was gone, and Shane was back in the hospital. The smell was just as he remembered it, and the tile floors clicked underfoot, making his steps sound like the clip-clopping of a horse.

Screams cut through the space from all sides. The rooms, silent when Shane had been held there, were now full of patients crying out in agony. Shane peered through the nearest window and saw a man with no legs and arms writhing on the floor. Blood seeped from the missing appendages and must have been doing so for ages. Stains upon stains lined the walls, from the freshest red near the bottom to brown and finally black as it reached chest height.

Shane crossed the hall to the next room and saw another patient strapped to a table. Thin wires, delicate like fishing line, were laced through his body and were holding his flesh open like the man's insides were on display. The skin was sliced and peeled from his face to his feet, exposing muscle, organs, and bone. Even his lips and eyelids had been peeled back, attached to the silver filaments, preventing him from speaking or closing his eyes. All he could do was scream.

Each room housed a single patient, a medical atrocity displayed in some perverse demonstration of cruelty. Shane knew they were not real, but they had come from the doctor's mind. They spoke volumes about the ghost Shane was dealing with.

Shane left the torture chambers behind, ignoring whatever waited in each subsequent room as he made his way to the end of the hall.

"Zircher," he yelled, running toward the exit.

The hallway continued well past where it should have ended. The longer Shane ran, the longer the hallway got, unfolding before him like it was being built before his eyes.

Screams continued from all corners. Cries of agony, pleas for mercy, an entire symphony of people in anguish. Shane ignored them, looking for the doctor, and eager to put an end to Hawkins' games.

A door opened behind him. Shane turned and saw that the first door he had looked in, far at the end of the hall now, had swung open. The armless, legless spirit squirmed out into the hall, gushing blood from the exposed wounds where its appendages had once been attached.

Other doors opened, clicking one after another. The spirit splayed open with wires ambled out into the hall, dragging the thin filaments behind it. More horrors walked or lurched or crawled out of their rooms, trailing blood and bits of flesh behind them. A handful at first, but then dozens flooded into the hall and made a beeline for Shane.

If one of them was the doctor, he couldn't tell. So many came at once that they would soon overwhelm him. Shane's patience was running thin. After the swamp ghost, he had played enough games with Hawkins' little toys. He didn't care who Dr. Zircher was, who he had been, or what his plans were.

Shane reached into his pocket. His fingers closed around a small glass jar. He had left most of what he'd found in the scrapyard back in the Escalade. Most, but not all of it. He hadn't needed anything until now.

He extended his arm and then let loose, throwing as hard as he could toward the oncoming menagerie of torture. The jar full of iron filings smashed on the floor, sending the bits of rusted metal scattering in all directions.

The hospital illusion was shattered. In the time it took Shane to blink, the hallway and all the bloody monstrosities were gone. He was once again in Hawkins' suite. Zircher reappeared a moment later, indicating Hawkins and the haunted item had not gotten far. He looked perturbed.

"You are resourceful," the doctor said. "That is ideal."

Shane came for him, and Zircher simply waited. He attacked the ghost quickly, wanting to put an end to him and be on his way before Hawkins could get out of the hotel. Despite his frail and old appearance, the doctor was not as weak as he seemed.

Zircher vanished into the nearest wall. The overhead lights flickered and died, and only the light from the windows, still mostly obscured by blinds, filled the room.

Shane had no reason to stick around to draw the ghost out. He pivoted quickly when Zircher retreated and instead headed for the door. Hawkins must have fled while Shane was distracted in the fake hospital, but that would have only given him a few minutes' head start.

"You have not been dismissed," Zircher said as Shane opened the door. The handle pulled free in his grasp, and the door slammed shut. Zircher appeared in Shane's path and lifted him from the floor by his throat, raising him until the doctor's arm was fully extended.

Shane kicked the ghost in the knee and caused him to stumble. He dropped Shane but did not hesitate before grabbing Shane again and pulling him close. Zircher was powerful, much stronger than the living man ever would have been, and he manhandled Shane like he was a child.

The doctor pulled Shane off of the ground and held him close from behind, his arm wrapped tightly around Shane's neck.

"If you are compliant, I can make it bearable," the doctor said. "I know every nerve of the human body. Every pathway to generate pain. I can make it so much worse for you if you force me to discipline you."

"Discipline? Doesn't sound very doctorly," Shane said. He struggled in Zircher's grip and the ghost's arm tightened, cutting off his airflow.

"You are an anomalous individual. I would take great personal satisfaction in learning how your brain works. If you are willing to concede, I will offer you the mercy of a pain-free death. Surely, that will appeal to you."

Shane opened his mouth, and Zircher relaxed just enough to allow him to speak. Rather than offering an answer, he sank his teeth into the ghost's wrist. Spongy, dead tissue gave way between his jaws, and he took the largest bite his mouth would allow, tearing deep into the phantom tissue.

Zircher cried out in surprise and pulled away, forcing the chunk of arm to break free. Shane stumbled away from the ghost and spit the chunk of meat back at him. It vanished almost immediately, but the wound it left did not. The scar would be permanent, for as long as the spirit existed.

"Then I will do as instructed. I will have to make this hurt very badly," the doctor said tersely.

Shane smiled but his potential response was silenced when the door behind him caught fire.

The scream that cut through the room forced him to cover his ears. It was shrill like a siren at close range, and he could barely stand being near it.

Fire crackled and wood snapped as the door immolated almost instantly, falling apart as Jackie Lantern stormed through it, trailing fire and smoke.

Dr. Zircher was stunned by the spirit's presence, a look of shock but also recognition on his face.

"Mr. Barbieri," Zircher said.

Jackie shrieked and rushed the other ghost, black hands trailing gouts of flame. Zircher tried to stop the spirit but was set alight with ghostly flame as soon as he made contact. His suit fell in flaming clumps while Jackie dug his burned fingers into the doctor's guts.

Shane moved away from the flames, no longer cold like they had been on the street, the heat searing his flesh. Zircher screamed, and soon Jackie Lantern's howls were not anguished screams, but peals of laughter.

Hugo slinked across the room from the door, ignoring Shane. While Zircher fought Jackie off, Hugo aided his flaming companion. With deft hands and brute strength, he tore off one of Zircher's feet at the ankle and then smashed the knee of his other leg, preventing any further assault with his lower body.

Fire consumed Zircher. Shane had never seen a ghost burned so thoroughly by another spirit's undead flames. It was causing real pain and real damage, but because Zircher was already dead, it couldn't kill him.

Hugo had said Jackie wanted revenge. And it seemed he did as well. It was why Hugo had agreed to come along. He had known Hawkins had taken Zircher's ghost. This would be his attempt to get back at his murderer. Shane couldn't be mad at him for keeping it a secret. He might have done the same thing.

"Hugo. Jackie," Shane shouted, knocking the burning embers from the ruined door. The flaming ghost shrieked but ignored him. Hugo, however, lifted his head. "Make it hurt."

Hugo grinned, and Jackie's laughter brought forth a new round of flaming vomit that poured over Dr. Zircher's screaming body. Shane left them to do their work. He could finish on his own, he just needed to find Captain Hawkins.

Shane ran back down the hall the way he had come and returned to the stairway. Jackie had burned all the doors in his travels but had set no permanent fires inside the building.

The stairwell was alive with sound when Shane reached it. People were evacuating lower floors, screaming and shouting as they went. He looked down over the railing and watched the flow of thirty floors of people running for their lives. He could see some figures heading in the other direction, however. Fleeting glimpses of black-gloved hands and tactical jackets. Men and women running up the stairs, fully armed and ready. The feds had gotten Shane's message.

With the elevators down and the FBI on their way up, Hawkins would have few options. One stood out in Shane's mind, though. He directed his eyes up. Hawkins had a helipad at his house, and Reapers seemed to love helicopters.

Shane headed up the stairs.

CHAPTER 27

WHAT GOES UP

Shane raced up the final few floors until he found the door marked for roof access. It was wired to set off an alarm if someone went out, but the hotel was full of alarms going off thanks to Jackie's fires. Combined with the sirens inside, no one would notice anything.

It was a hot day, and the roof was fully exposed to the sun. Shane was not sure where the police helicopter had gone, but the skies were empty save for the rising smoke from 42nd Street as he stepped out of the stairwell and closed the door behind him.

He could see no sign of Hawkins on the roof. There were too many electrical boxes, exposed bits of ductwork, and a second door with access on the far side of the roof for Shane to get a clear view of anything happening around him. Too many places to hide. There was, however, a helipad in the center of the roof.

Shane did a quick sweep of the area near the door and saw nothing. He stepped away slowly, moving toward the helipad, and circled wide of some aluminum ducts. On the far side, Hawkins stood with his briefcase in one hand and a phone pressed to his ear in the other.

"Then go there in person," he spat, angry with whomever he was speaking. "Empty them all, close them out, I don't care. Get the money and meet me there."

"Closing your accounts?" Shane interrupted. "That doesn't sound like a good business move."

Hawkins inhaled sharply, backing away from Shane as he dropped his briefcase and reached into his suit jacket. Shane ran at him, tackling him at the waist before he could draw the gun. They landed hard, but Hawkins was quick to slam his phone on Shane's head, smashing it with enough force to split the flesh on his scalp.

"Jesus Christ, does nothing kill you?" Hawkins growled. He hammered his fist down on Shane's ear and temple while Shane returned the favor, driving a fist into Hawkins' kidneys and ribs.

Blood ran down Shane's face from the gash on his head. He shook himself over Hawkins, painting him red and causing him to flinch and turn away as drops of blood fell into his eyes and mouth. The distraction was enough to allow Shane to alter his position and drive a knee as hard as he could into the other man's groin.

Hawkins groaned in pain and thrashed his body, rolling to one side and forcing Shane to move with him. They landed face to face, and Hawkins went for his gun again.

"I'm getting off this rooftop, Ryan. I'm going to kill you, and I'll be in Canada with a fortune before the sun sets."

Shane grabbed his wrists as the two of them wrestled over the weapon. Shane heard the distant sound of a helicopter approaching. Hawkins would have backup soon.

Hawkins had a solid grip on the gun, but Shane squeezed the man's hands, trying to crush bones. The former captain struggled and jerked his arm wildly, and Shane took a gamble by letting go.

The gun flew, hitting the helipad and skittering across it toward the edge of the roof where it clattered against the wall. Hawkins cursed and jammed his finger into the gash he'd opened on Shane's head, digging into the split flesh, and scraping his thumbnail on the wound.

Shane screamed and Hawkins kicked him away, turning and scrambling into a crawl as he got to his feet. Shane was after him in a second, barely out of arm's reach as they raced toward the gun.

Hawkins dove, grabbing the gun, and rolling into a crouch. He fired a shot, narrowly missing Shane and stopping him dead. A mere handful of feet separated them, but Hawkins could squeeze the trigger before Shane took a single step.

"You can follow direction, look at that," Hawkins said, rising to his feet.

He gestured at Shane with the gun, and Shane raised his hands. The helicopter was approaching from the downtown area, and the sirens below sounded hollow and distended as they echoed up the sides of buildings to the rooftop.

"I only wanted Dr. Loomis to scramble those brains. Guess I'm going to have to blow them clean out of your skull."

He raised the gun higher, and Shane gritted his teeth. The sound of the blast sent a chill like ice down his spine, and he closed his eyes, feeling his entire body tense.

Hawkins screamed. The pain and darkness of death did not come for Shane. He opened his eyes and watched as Hawkins collapsed backward in slow motion, the gun falling from his hand.

His right leg spun away from his body as though it had been snapped off and kicked aside. A spray of blood blossomed in the air around his waist. Scraps of his pants soaked in blood splattered across Shane's face.

Shane stared, dumbfounded, for a heartbeat. Hawkins' leg landed a couple of feet from the rest of his body, the upper thigh mangled and still twitching as the ragged, ugly stump gushed blood onto the hotel roof.

"You put it in your pocket," Shane said.

Hawkins was gasping, his back against the wall overlooking 42nd Street, bracing himself as the wound from his leg pumped blood. He had stashed Zircher's haunted item in his pocket before he left the hotel suite. Jackie and Hugo must have finished the job.

Shane approached Hawkins. He was bleeding profusely, the artery in his leg like a faucet. At best, he had minutes to live.

Hawkins watched as Shane came for him, gasping and clutching at the wall, his face a mask of pain.

"You're a son of a bitch, you know that?" Hawkins choked.

"So are you," Shane told him.

Hawkins growled, pain and anger mixing on his face as he shook his head.

"You think you won? You gonna watch me die? I had you dead to rights. You didn't win. You didn't even kill me. You got lucky!" he spat.

Shane took another step, looming over the man and then peering over the edge of the building. Police had set up a barricade on the street below. Flaming cars were being put out by fire crews. The street looked relatively empty.

"Who said I didn't kill you?" Shane asked.

The helicopter thundered overhead as it approached the rooftop. Shane could see a man inside, armed and ready, with the door open. He grabbed Hawkins by his shirtfront and pulled him to the edge of the wall.

"No," Hawkins growled, weakly trying to pull Shane's hands free.

"Enjoy your flight," Shane said. He hauled Hawkins up to the edge and let go.

Blood slicked the edge of the wall, and the captain cursed as he fell from Shane's grip. He didn't scream on the way down.

The helicopter hovered in place for a long moment. Shane was about to go for Hawkins' gun when the chopper pulled away sharply, fleeing the area. Within seconds, the roof was flooded with federal agents.

Shane raised his hands as a dozen men and women in blue jackets emblazoned with yellow "FBI" letters across the back drew on him and surrounded him. Half a dozen more shouted orders and secured the area as Shane was forced to his knees, a gun firmly on the back of his head as he was handcuffed.

Blood poured down his face from the scalp wound, and he must have looked like a monster. The police helicopter reappeared moments later, following the escaping Reapers.

Agents talked on radios, talked to each other, and yelled at people

Shane couldn't see.

"Hope you can explain all of this," a familiar voice asked.

Shane lifted his head and looked up at a man in a dark suit and sunglasses. FBI Special Agent Xander Ventura looked tired and nervous.

"Agent Ventura. Fancy seeing you here," Shane said.

"Yes, very fancy." Ventura pulled Shane to his feet and took off the handcuffs.

"Can we get a medic here?" he shouted at no one in particular.

"I'm fine," Shane said.

"Your face is a mask of death, I can see your skull, and there's a leg lying on the roof next to you."

"It's not mine," Shane said.

"No, I see that. Any idea where the owner is?"

"Try 42nd Street," Shane answered.

Ventura sighed loudly then leaned in close so only Shane could hear.

"You're not making this easy," he said.

Ventura's ability to see ghosts meant he would understand the case better than anyone. It also meant he'd likely do some quick thinking to keep Shane out of trouble. But throwing their suspect off the roof was probably not what he'd hoped for.

"It wasn't me. Honestly. His leg exploded on its own."

"On its own?" Ventura asked dubiously. Shane shrugged.

"The man was into some shady stuff."

Ventura pulled away as a medic approached and forced Shane to sit as he inspected his head wound.

"You're going to have to answer a hell of a lot of questions," Ventura said.

"Figured as much."

"He'll need to get to a hospital to get this treated," the medic added after applying a temporary bandage.

"Sure. Yeah. I'll go with him."

Ventura led Shane back to the stairwell and down the stairs. By the time they got to the street, Shane was a little lightheaded and thought maybe a hospital wasn't a terrible idea.

"So, is this mess done now?" Ventura asked, getting into an ambulance with Shane.

The car fires had all been put out, though the bus was still a smoking heap that firefighters kept blasting with water. Police and agents were everywhere, and the media had created a wall of cameras and trucks outside the barricaded area.

"Sure as hell hope so," Shane said.

The sirens screamed to life, and cars parted to let the ambulance pass. Shane tried to light a cigarette, but the paramedic took it from him and threw it on the floor. He could wait for when everything was calm.

EPILOGUE

The day was blazing hot, and there was not a cloud in the sky to offer relief from the sun. Shane stood on the porch, squinting and barely able to see the man in front of him. The sun burned the stitched wound on the top of his head, but he ignored it.

"You have no idea what kind of magic I had to conjure to pull this off," Agent Ventura said.

"You're good at your job," Herbert said.

Ventura wore a black suit, and his forehead was beaded with sweat. Shane was keeping in the sun only out of the vaguest sense of amusement. It was better that Ventura didn't come into the house, anyway. Eloise was still on edge, and Ventura didn't look like he needed the stress.

"I'm serious, Ryan. You can't pop up on my radar again for, like, twenty years. Someone's going to start asking questions about us."

"You weren't even involved," Shane said.

"I wasn't until I was. Until you sent me those files from Hawkins' computer. Then it became my case. My second case with you in the center of it, and a series of events I have to explain with the most paper-thin lies. Take it easy, please. For my sake."

"I'll try," Shane said.

Ventura had proven a reliable and trustworthy ally. The man could see ghosts, but as a federal agent, he could make a lot more happen in an official capacity than Shane could, even if he had to sweep a lot of truth under the rug.

Ventura had flipped the script on Hawkins' and Dr. Loomis' lies about Shane. Like several other former members of units Hawkins had worked with in the military, Shane was officially just one more victim of a disgraced Marine captain who had been making treasonous deals with foreign governments to misappropriate U.S. military assets. He ran a mercenary company, killers for hire, and either murdered those who crossed him, like Davis Blakely, or framed them, like Shane Ryan.

Ventura assured Shane that the details were solid enough that no one would question the story too deeply. If they did, they'd run up against inconsistencies on Hawkins' end, like the spectral assets. Things that made Hawkins and the brass of the Reaper Company look like madmen. Shane was exonerated. But that didn't mean people higher up the food chain than Ventura wouldn't remember his name if they saw it again.

"I appreciate what you did, Ventura. Thank you," Shane said.

He extended his hand, and the agent shook it.

"Honestly, the government owes you a debt on this one. Ghosts or not, Hawkins stole millions in equipment and was set to stage a coup down south. This was a good outcome."

"And everyone lived," Herbert added.

"Not really," Shane clarified. He had not filled Herbert or the others in on what happened.

"You lived," Herbert said.

"What about the rest of the Reapers in Europe?" Shane asked.

"In custody or on the run," Ventura said. "There weren't many left. Assets have been seized, so there's not much hope for the few who got away. If we can't round them up, they'll be alone and rogue, just a few random mercenaries with ghosts in the darkest corners of the world."

"Good," Shane said. "How about Hugo and Jackie Lantern?"

"Your psychopath ghost friends? I took that knife you gave me back to the hospital and buried it on the grounds. He said you should come by sometime."

"Of course. And the other one?"

"Gone. Found the box outside of the juice bar, but there was nothing in it."

Shane grunted. Someone had stolen the haunted item of a blazing psychopath ghost. Just one more reason to avoid New York.

He was glad to be done with them, all things being equal, and hoped that would be the end of it. Mostly, he was relieved that the Reapers had been put down. The world didn't need ghost mercenaries. It had enough problems.

"I have to get back to Washington, but, you know, keep out of trouble," Ventura said, putting on a pair of sunglasses that made him look like a complete stereotype. Shane chuckled and watched him leave.

"You two would make a good team," Herbert said. "Did you ever consider becoming a police officer or an FBI agent?"

Shane laughed again and entered the house with the big ghost trailing behind him. Herbert was definitely new to the house.

"All is well, I trust," Carl said as Shane closed the door. The German ghost stood stiffly next to the grandfather clock. The Davis sisters were nearby as well, as was Thaddeus. Eloise stood at the forefront, her arms crossed over her chest as she stared at Shane with her sunken eyes.

"All is well," Shane confirmed.

He passed them all by and made his way to the kitchen, where he put on a pot of water to make coffee. The ghosts filtered into the room around him, making the space seem much more crowded than it should have been. He sometimes wondered what it was like to live alone, even though there was no one else alive in the house with him.

"Will those men be coming back to the house?" Daisy asked. "Do we need to go out and fight anyone?"

"I don't think anyone is coming back," Shane answered.

He retrieved a cigarette from the pack in his pocket and lit it while the others watched and waited patiently as though he were on a stage about to engage in a great speech. Shane took a long puff and then exhaled smoke, glancing at each of the spirits in turn.

"Well, what happened?" Eloise demanded. "You leave, you almost die, we get swarmed by strange men and ghosts, you come back, and leave *again*! This is hardly a civilized way to run a household."

Shane took another puff and nodded.

"I'm going to have my coffee first if you don't mind," he said. "There's plenty of time to fill you in. I'm not going anywhere."

Carl's smile was barely noticeable, but Eloise remained defiant.

"Aren't you? How do I know that? What if tomorrow, you have to go fight, oh, I don't know, some vampires in Romania?"

"Are there really vampires in Romania?" Herbert asked excitedly.

Shane took a mug from the cupboard and set it on the counter. He set about making himself coffee, and when it was ready, he placed it on the table and sat down. The ghosts watched him while he took the first tentative sip.

"There is plenty of time," he said again.

❦

Check out these best-selling series from our talented authors:

GHOST STORIES

RON RIPLEY
BERKLEY STREET SERIES
MOVING IN SERIES
HAUNTED COLLECTION SERIES
DEATH HUNTER SERIES

IAN FORTEY
JIGSAW OF SOULS SERIES
CULT OF THE ENDLESS NIGHT SERIES

SUPERNATURAL SUSPENSE

A. I. NASSER
SLAUGHTER SERIES
SIN SERIES

DAVID LONGHORN
NIGHTMARE SERIES
ASYLUM SERIES

SARA CLANCY
THE BELL WITCH SERIES
BANSHEE SERIES

For a complete list of our new releases and best-selling horror books, visit ScareStreet.com or scan the QR code below!

www.ingramcontent.com/pod-product-compliance
Lightning Source LLC
Chambersburg PA
CBHW050344030726
47503CB00008B/2612